## "A fifty-fifty split?"

To Allie's surprise, he actually seemed to think it over.

"After expenses, of course. It's a win-win situation. A sensible choice for us both." Especially if she could find a way to convince Cooper he didn't really want to run a fishing charter.

Suddenly he smiled, and his face transformed. Her heart gave a little lurch. Oh, my, he was ten times more good-looking when he smiled.

"I guess that would make us partners," he said with an unexpected twinkle in his eye that made Allie's stomach swoop.

Maybe she should have thought this over first.

Dear Reader,

Texas is a lot more than ranches and cowboys, cactus and coyotes. My home state has mountains, cosmopolitan cities, thick pine forests and moody swamps, all of which I have used as settings in my books. But one of my favorite places to visit is the Texas Gulf Coast. I love the slow, Margaritaville pace of life in the small coastal towns, the sunny beaches, the fresh seafood.

What better place to have a romance?

The town of Port Clara is entirely fictitious, an amalgam of actual towns I've visited. But it has become so real to me, I half expect to see it on the Texas map.

I hope you enjoy getting to know Port Clara through the eyes of two people who love it as much as I do—Cooper and Allie, who get to fall in love there.

Best,

Kara Lennox

# Reluctant Partners
## Kara Lennox

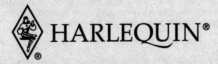

HARLEQUIN®

TORONTO • NEW YORK • LONDON
AMSTERDAM • PARIS • SYDNEY • HAMBURG
STOCKHOLM • ATHENS • TOKYO • MILAN • MADRID
PRAGUE • WARSAW • BUDAPEST • AUCKLAND

ISBN-13: 978-0-373-75220-1
ISBN-10:    0-373-75220-2

RELUCTANT PARTNERS

www.eHarlequin.com

**Printed in U.S.A.**

# ABOUT THE AUTHOR

Texas native Kara Lennox has earned her living at various times as an art director, typesetter, textbook editor and reporter. She's worked in a boutique, a health club and an ad agency. She's been an antiques dealer and even a blackjack dealer. But no work has made her happier than writing romance novels. She has written more than fifty books.

When not writing, Kara indulges in an ever-changing array of hobbies. Her latest passions are bird-watching and long-distance bicycling. She loves to hear from readers; you can visit her Web page at www.karalennox.com.

## Books by Kara Lennox

### HARLEQUIN AMERICAN ROMANCE

For Captain Bombay Flares of the *Terminator* in Kona, Hawaii, who patiently answered my questions about fishing while cleaning a tuna

# Chapter One

Standing on the dock at the Port Clara Marina, Cooper Remington gave his inheritance a long, leisurely inspection, his gaze roaming from stem to stern. He couldn't believe he was really back, after all these years.

"It's kinda beat up." This observation came from Max, Cooper's cousin and now one of his partners.

"It's a disaster." Reece, the third Remington cousin, shook his head and gazed down at his oxfords. "I told you guys we should have looked into this further before flying down to Texas half-cocked."

"All right, so the *Dragonfly* needs a little work," Cooper said. He wasn't blind to the rust and peeling paint. "That's to be expected. Uncle Johnny was sick the last few months of his life, and he had a drinking problem before that. He probably wasn't able to paint and scrub barnacles. But we can do that stuff."

Cooper, the oldest of the cousins at thirty-six, was the optimist of the group. Though saddened by Uncle Johnny's death, Cooper's mind had filled with possibilities the moment he'd learned that he and his two cousins had inherited the *Dragonfly*.

He loved the ocean, loved boats and sailing. And he was sick to death of corporate law, the field he'd gone into because his family had expected it. Cooper and his cousins, equally disillusioned with their second-son, second-class jobs in the family corporation, could make a lot of money running a fishing charter and have fun doing it.

That was the theory, anyway.

"I guess it wouldn't hurt to go aboard," Reece said, his face a bit green. Reece didn't much care for boats. Didn't like cars, trains or planes, either. He never traveled anywhere without his Dramamine.

Max wasn't paying attention to the *Dragonfly,* but to the sleek pleasure yacht in the next slip, where a woman in a bikini was sweeping the deck.

"Max." Cooper nudged his cousin. "We're boarding." They didn't yet have keys, so they couldn't inspect the inside. But they could check out whatever was in plain sight.

As he unfastened the chain that blocked the gangway and stepped on board, the years melted away and he was once again a boy looking forward to weeks of fishing and swimming and helping Uncle Johnny and Aunt Pat run their fishing trips.

That was before Aunt Pat died, before Uncle Johnny had started drinking, before the family had decided Johnny wasn't fit company for impressionable youngsters.

Before Uncle Johnny, smarting from the snub, had cut off all contact with his family.

The close-up look didn't improve the *Dragonfly*'s condition. Max and Reece were right—the boat was in bad shape. But some good, hard physical labor was just what Cooper needed, what all of them needed, to cleanse the corporate rat race out of their systems.

"It's smaller than I remember," Reece observed.

"You're just bigger," Cooper replied. "How old were you last time you were on this boat? Ten?"

"Thirteen, that last summer." Reece laughed unexpectedly. "I barfed all over Uncle Johnny's customer *and* his prize tuna. That was great."

Cooper had been fifteen when his parents had declared an end to summer vacations with Uncle Johnny. It hadn't seemed right to leave Johnny to grieve and drink alone, but his parents had held firm. He'd thought there would be other summers, but Johnny had never again invited his nephews to visit.

"Ahh." Max's sigh of pleasure jerked Cooper back to the present. His youngest cousin had already found himself a place to sit and bask in the sun. "All I need is a frozen daiquiri and a couple of babes in bikinis." He glanced over his shoulder at the yacht in the next slip, but the bikini-woman had disappeared.

Cooper jumped on his cousin's weakness, using it to his advantage. "And you'll have that. Once we get her polished up, the *Dragonfly* will be a babe magnet."

"But can she support you and Max?" Reece asked. "Have you crunched the numbers?"

Cooper's enthusiasm could not be dimmed by facts and figures—or their absence. "Are you kidding? She can support all three of us. You know what we have here?"

Reece arched one eyebrow. "A money pit?"

"A license to print money. We can charge thousands of dollars for each excursion. Max, with your sales and marketing experience you can bring in the high-rolling customers in droves. And, Reece, you can keep the business on track financially."

"And you'll be the captain?" Max asked, giving his cousin a dubious look.

"Yeah. Aw, hell, I don't care about that. We can take turns if you want. But we'll be equal partners. We won't have to kowtow to our fathers and older brothers anymore." The Remington clan was blessed—or cursed—with a surplus of male heirs brimming with ambition and testosterone.

Reece shook his head. "I'll get the finances straightened out and set up the books, but then I'm gone."

Max grinned. "Well, *I'm* in. I didn't leave any doors open when I resigned. In fact, my father's not talking to me."

Cooper hadn't exactly left Remington Industries with a lot of warm fuzzies, either. Technically his father, vice president of legal affairs, was still speaking to him but saying things like, "You've gone completely off your nut" and "Don't expect to come crawling back and step into your old job." His mother simply wept every time they talked, sobbing about all the money they'd wasted on his Harvard law degree.

They'd get over it. Cooper wished Reece had quit, too, instead of taking vacation time, which he'd been saving up for years because he thought vacations were a waste. If anybody needed to learn how to kick back and enjoy life, it was Reece. The guy was strung tighter than a sail in a hurricane.

Cooper checked his watch. "Almost nine o'clock. Let's see if the marina's open yet."

He turned toward the gangway just as a feminine shriek behind him made him nearly leap out of his skin. He whirled around and found himself face to face with…a red-headed vision. Barefoot, and with long, tanned arms and legs fetchingly displayed in low-slung shorts and a cropped T-shirt, she was absolutely, heart-stoppingly gorgeous.

But, boy, was she mad.

"What are you doing on my boat?" She took a menacing step forward, a heavy ceramic coffee cup clutched between her hands. Cooper had no doubt she could do damage with it. "You can't just board somebody's boat without permission. Now get the hell off! I've got a gun below and I'm using it if you're not gone in five seconds."

Cooper's respect for the woman crept up a notch. What an amazing creature, fierce and vulnerable at the same time. He knew he should heed her warning, but he stood rooted to the spot, unable to tear his gaze away. She'd rendered him speechless, too. No intelligent explanations occurred to him.

ALLIE BATEMAN WAS SCARED out of her wits, but she was trying hard not to show it. She'd been warned about living alone on the *Dragonfly,* warned that beach communities drew predators as well as tourists. But she hadn't actually believed anything bad would happen to her until now.

These guys shouldn't have felt menacing in their *GQ* weekend casual clothes. But there was something about the man in front—a keen determination in the thrust of his jaw—that made her uneasy.

He seemed to shake himself. "Who are you?"

At least her uninvited guests didn't appear to be set on immediate raping and pillaging, so Allie changed tack. "I'm Allie Bateman. Are you looking for a fishing charter?" No sense driving away perfectly good business, if that's what it was. These guys for sure weren't local, not with those clothes and Yankee accents. Were they here for a wild weekend of drinking and womanizing?

She studied the leader of the pack again. He didn't look the type to overindulge. His body showed no signs of softness, no paunch from too many three-martini lunches and fatty steaks.

The man returned her scrutiny. "No, we're not here to book a charter."

"Then why are you on my boat?" Prickles of apprehension tickled her scalp, and this time it had nothing to do with fear of bodily harm.

"The question isn't what we're doing on your boat, it's what are *you* doing on ours? I'm Cooper Remington, and these are my cousins Reece and Max. This *is* Johnny Remington's boat, right?"

Her heart still squeezed painfully every time she thought of Johnny, of how valiantly he fought his illness right down to the end, how he never complained about the pain though she knew it must have been horrific. Then the interloper's name registered.

She sucked in a breath. "Johnny Remington passed away a couple of months ago. I'm the new owner." Just what she didn't need—concerned family, conveniently late to help, but just in time to grab what they could.

The one called Cooper narrowed his eyes. "Um, 'fraid not. Johnny's will, filed in a New York State court, left the boat to us. We're his nephews. So whatever arrangements he made with you are null and void."

"Null and void? Really?" She cocked her head to one side. "Are you by any chance a lawyer?"

"I am, but that's immaterial."

Allie's hackles rose. "I knew it. I can spot lawyers from miles away." She'd been afraid this would happen. The powerful Remingtons wouldn't just let a valuable asset like the *Dragonfly* fall into a stranger's hands without a fight.

She flashed back in time to another boat, another slick

lawyer, another disagreement about who owned what. Allie had lost that battle. But she didn't intend to lose this one. Though Johnny's will was handwritten, it had been witnessed and she felt certain it was entirely legal.

She crossed her arms. "Johnny's more recent will, filed in the state of Texas, names me as the one to inherit the *Dragonfly*. So get off *my* boat."

"And just who might you be?"

"For the second time, my name is Allie Bateman."

"And what's your relationship to Johnny?"

She could have told him that Johnny was her employer for more than ten years. He'd been her teacher, her father-figure, and her dear, dear friend. But she knew what this guy was thinking—that she was some floozy who'd somehow fleeced Johnny out of his boat when he'd been sick and feeble.

Let him think whatever he wanted. "That's none of your business."

"Hey, Allie!" The greeting was from Jane Simone, her next-door neighbor. "Is everything okay?"

Allie gave Cooper a pointed look. "*Is* everything okay? Or should I tell Jane to call the cops?"

Cooper's blue eyes flashed. Obviously he enjoyed crossing swords. "I'll bring my own cops. When I come back with a judge's order for you to vacate."

"Good thinking. Run that New York attitude against a Texas judge and see where it gets you."

Cooper Remington gave her one last, appraising look before turning and stalking away, taking his gang with him. She watched until they climbed into a silver BMW and drove away.

"What was that about?" Jane asked.

"Trouble. Jane, I'm afraid I'm in big, big trouble."

Her heart hammered inside her chest as she made her way into the galley and set her cooling coffee on the counter. Her visitors had shaken her more than she wanted to admit.

She was in the right, she had to be. Johnny had wanted *her* to have the boat. She'd put a lot of her own money into the upkeep as Johnny's worsening illness forced him to cut back on excursions, and most of the rest of her savings had gone into the boat during the months after his death. She'd asked him if his family would mind that he was giving his boat to her, and he said his family didn't even acknowledge him.

But when it comes to inheriting money or valuables, relatives came out of the woodwork. Just because she was legally entitled to the *Dragonfly* didn't mean she would get it. Mr. L.L. Bean out there probably had some deep pockets. He probably had an army of lawyer buddies and a whole slew of legal tricks to defraud her out of her livelihood so he and his cousins could…God knew what. Probably sell the *Dragonfly* to the highest bidder and run off to the Riviera with the proceeds, or use it as their personal party boat and run it aground.

Against that, she had zero money and one septuagenarian, semi-retired lawyer, the one who'd filed the will for her and promised her it was legal.

The odds weren't in her favor. But she wouldn't go down without a fight.

COOPER AND REECE SAT ON the beachfront patio of Old Salt's Bar & Grill, one of a handful of eateries that lined the beach around Port Clara's main dock and marina. Max had slipped away somewhere. Cooper suspected his younger cousin's disappearance might have something to do with pretty, bikini-clad Jane, Allie Bateman's neighbor. Max was a smart guy, consistently Remington Industries' top sales executive. But when it came to beautiful women, he lost his ability to reason.

"So, what do you think?" Reece asked.

"I think she's gorgeous," Cooper automatically replied. Okay, so Max wasn't the only one whose head could be turned by a pretty girl.

Reece's jaw dropped. "The *Dragonfly?* She's a wreck."

"I was talking about Allie Bateman."

"Oh." Reece took off his glasses and absently polished them with his napkin. "I suppose she's okay, but what does that have to do with anything? She's on our boat. Do you think she's telling the truth?"

"Unlikely." In his experience, beautiful young women like Allie didn't have to rely on honesty. They used their physical assets to subdue a guy's natural defenses, then manipulated facts and situations to suit their desires. "I'll call a legal researcher I know in Austin and have him check out this supposed will. But my first inclination is to believe it's bogus. Allie's not even a blood relation."

"Maybe she's not related to Johnny, but I doubt she's a stranger," Reece pointed out. "She was probably his girlfriend."

Cooper curled his lip in distaste. He didn't want to picture his seventy-something-year-old uncle and young, vibrant Allie Bateman…blech.

"Maybe even his common-law wife," Reece added.

Cooper took a long sip of his coffee as he contemplated the gentle waves lapping at the beach below. "He wouldn't have changed his will."

"Why not? None of us have seen him in years."

"Maybe not. But I sent him a Christmas present every year. Sometimes he sent me a card. I wonder why he didn't tell anyone he had cancer?"

"Would you have rushed down here to take care of him if you'd known?" Reece asked. "Would any of us? Last I heard, my dad and Johnny weren't speaking."

"I'm not sure what the beef was between Uncle Johnny and the rest of the family, but he wasn't mad at you or me or Max. He wouldn't have disinherited us without a damn good reason."

"Maybe he wanted to take care of Allie."

"And maybe Allie took advantage of a sick old man and conned him into changing his will."

The waitress chose then to bring out their breakfasts. Reece frowned at his bowl of oatmeal, then picked the raisins out one by one, replacing them with strawberries. Cooper dug into his bacon and eggs.

"Not all women are Heather, you know," Reece said, almost absently.

Cooper gritted his teeth. "Don't bring her into this."

A few moments later Max joined them, his face carefully turned away. He pulled out one of the wooden chairs and swiveled it around so he could straddle it.

"Good God, man, what happened to you?" Cooper demanded when he spotted the plastic bag of ice Max held against his face.

Max didn't seem to be suffering much. He grinned. "Remember Allie's neighbor Jane? Well, the woman has a jealous husband with a mean left hook."

Reece looked up, horrified, but Cooper took it in stride. "Max, when are you going to learn to ask first? Someday a jealous husband is going to do more than blacken your eye."

Max sighed. "She's gorgeous. The guy said he'd kill me if I so much as looked at her again. How am I going to not look at her if she's on the boat next to ours?"

"You'll be too busy," Cooper replied. "We need to launch a massive advertising and marketing campaign for Remington Charters. Sure you're up to it?"

Max perked up. "Absolutely. When do we start?"

"As soon as I can evict one redhead, we're good to go."

"You're not just going to pitch her out in the street, are you?" Reece asked. "What if she doesn't have anywhere else to go?"

"Not my problem."

Max didn't look happy. "I thought you were tired of being a ruthless SOB. What happened to the kinder, gentler Cooper?"

"He's waiting for his damned boat."

## Chapter Two

"Your account is overdue, Miss Allie." Dino the grocer said this pleasantly enough as he rang up her current purchases early Monday morning, but a thread of worry underlay his reminder.

A lot of people had voiced doubts that she could continue to run the charter service by herself. When Johnny had been strong and vibrant—until as recently as a couple of years ago, in fact—Remington Charters had made plenty of money, enough that Johnny could cover his bills and pay Allie a decent salary. He'd also allowed her to sleep in the V-berth, which meant she had socked away savings instead of spending all her salary on rent.

But as Johnny had weakened, so had the finances. Johnny had urged her to find another job where she could earn what she was worth, but she hadn't even considered leaving him, not when he had no family to take care of him. Pat, his only love, had died many years ago. They'd never had kids, and he'd never remarried.

So she'd stuck by him, took care of him and buried him. Once a decent interval had passed, she'd started taking on charter trips again, after spending more than she could afford to have both engines rebuilt. But business was sparse, and she couldn't take on the large parties like before—she couldn't coach more than four fishermen *and* serve snacks *and* captain the boat.

Still, the busy tourist season was about to begin and she was optimistic that she could turn a financial corner soon. Once she cleared the most immediate debts and did some maintenance on the boat, she could hire an assistant, get the Web site back up, do some advertising.

If she still had a boat.

"I've got a lucrative charter this afternoon," she told Dino as she signed her name for today's groceries. "You're next on my list to pay."

Dino smiled and didn't question her further about the bill. She was as good as her word, and he knew it. "You're a brave girl, running that boat all by yourself. Why don't you get a husband to help you out?"

She rolled her eyes. Lots of well-meaning friends and acquaintances had voiced similar suggestions. "You send me a good-looking guy who knows how to sail—or an average-looking one who can cook and clean—I'll consider marrying him." As if guys were standing in line.

She wondered if Cooper Remington knew how to sail. He at least had the good-looking part down.

Dino bagged her fruit so as not to bruise it. "I hear some of Johnny's family showed up. They checked into Miss Greer's place."

Miss Greer ran the nicest B and B in town, the Sunsetter, located in one of the few Victorians that time and hurricanes hadn't obliterated. And, yes, Allie had heard that the trio of nephews hadn't been at all intimidated by her brave words from Friday morning. Though she hadn't heard another peep out of them over the weekend, it looked as if they were hunkering down, ready for a fight.

She'd made an appointment with Arlen Caldwell, her attorney, for tomorrow morning just to be sure her legal ducks were in a row, and to shore up any possible defenses against Cooper Remington's tricks.

"They aren't giving you any trouble, are they, Miss Allie? 'Cause if they are, I'll send Robert to talk to them." Robert was Dino's Goliath-sized son, who usually had a job as a bouncer in one or another of the bars in Port Clara.

"They're definitely here to give me trouble." She gathered up her bags of groceries. "But it's the kind that fists and strong words won't solve. So I appreciate the offer, but we better hold off siccing Robert on them."

"The offer holds. Any time." Dino made a fist and punched the air.

If Cooper and his gang succeeded in taking her boat away from her, maybe she'd unleash Robert. The fantasy gave her little comfort as she loaded her modest grocery purchase into the back of her Isuzu Rodeo.

Once upon a time, she and Johnny had offered all-day cruises including a gourmet lunch with wine. Nowadays her customers got tasty snacks—fresh fruit, bagels and cream cheese, bakery cookies and soft drinks.

She made another stop at the Quicky Mart for ice and drinks. The convenience store didn't offer her credit, so she had to pay cash from her dwindling reserves. She tried not to worry; she had several charters scheduled over the next couple of weeks, which would pull her fanny out of the fire.

She parked her Rodeo in her regular spot at the marina and grabbed the ice first, so she could get it to the ice chest where she would store drinks and snacks. The fishermen could help themselves that way. But as she made her way down the dock in her flip-flops toward the *Dragonfly,* she spotted Deputy Thom Casey leaning casually against a pylon near her slip, and her heart went into overdrive.

This wasn't good. Not good at all.

Thom had asked her out once. She'd turned him down—not because he wasn't a handsome or nice enough guy, but because he didn't sail and she couldn't afford the distraction of an actual social life.

She hoped he wouldn't hold that against her.

He saw her coming and stood up straighter, looking decidedly uncomfortable. So this wasn't a chance encounter.

"Hey, Thom, what's up?" she asked, noticing that her voice quavered.

"Hey, Allie. Sorry to greet you first thing in the morning with bad news."

"Bad news? Did someone die?" She didn't have any family left, but she had a lot of friends in Port Clara.

"A different kind of bad news. I have to deliver this injunction to you. It's a freeze on the *Dragonfly.* Because it's an asset of which the ownership is now in dispute, it's being impounded."

Allie dropped her bags of ice with a thud. She'd expected something, but not something this fast or this extreme.

"What does that mean, exactly?"

"If it were a car, it would be towed to an impound lot until ownership could be determined. But that's kind of hard to do with a boat. So this order specifies that the *Dragonfly* can't leave her slip."

She could feel the blood draining from her face. "I have charters all week!"

"I know, Allie. I hope you realize I had nothing to do with this. I'm just doing my job."

"Oh, Thom, I don't blame you. It's that jerk lawyer, Cooper Remington. Do I have to vacate the boat?" That was a frightening thought. A tiny berth on the *Dragonfly* wasn't much, but it was the only home she had. She didn't have enough ready assets in her personal account for even a month's rent for an efficiency apartment.

"No mention of that. In some cases like this, they would put a locking device on the boat's ignition so the engines couldn't even be started. But I don't think Judge Isaacs was willing to go for anything like that. He knows if there's a court order, you'll obey it."

"Of course I will, but why did they do this? I understand they want to get their hands on my boat, but what would it hurt if I kept working while this gets sorted out?"

Thom shrugged. "I haven't met the guy, so I don't know." He held out the court order. She took it and shoved it into her straw tote bag without reading it.

"I'm really sorry," Thom said. "If there's anything I can do…"

"That's really nice of you to offer." She noticed then that the *Princess II*—Jane and Scott's boat next door—looked as if it had been closed up tight. "What happened to the Simones?" she asked. "They were here Friday. I thought they were staying through this week."

Again, Thom shrugged. "No idea."

Deflated, Allie said goodbye to Thom and boarded the *Dragonfly,* dragging her now useless ice. She would have to hunt down another fishing boat and captain for the party she expected in a couple of hours. She felt terrible about disappointing some of her most loyal customers. It had taken

Johnny many years to build a reputation as a quality, reliable charter service. Even when they'd downsized, they'd been careful to never promise what they couldn't deliver.

It wouldn't take too many canceled trips for word to get around that she was a flake and the business was down the tubes.

Allie put away the groceries, then headed down the long dock to find an idle fishing boat, her heart heavy. But only a few footsteps later, she skidded to a stop. Maybe there was another way. She would have to swallow all the vitriol she longed to hurl at Cooper Remington and make nice, but if it meant the difference between failure and survival, she'd do it. She turned around and headed for her car.

Normally she would just walk the seven or eight blocks to the Sunsetter B and B. But time was of the essence. So she drove through the sleepy streets of Port Clara. In another few weeks the place would be teeming with tourists. Front Street, which paralleled the beach, would be closed off to car traffic and filled curb-to-curb with pedestrians. She relished the relative quiet, when it was mostly just the locals and the snowbirds. But tourists were the lifeblood of this place, so she welcomed them, too.

The Sunsetter B and B was a beautiful yet quirky redbrick Victorian two blocks off Front Street on Magnolia Lane. Although it did not have a view of the ocean, it was a lovely place to stay, sheltered as it was by a grove of coconut palms and surrounded by bougainvillea.

When Allie was a little girl, she'd been scared of Miss Greer. But she'd soon learned that the stern widow had a soft spot for anybody who needed a cookie.

Years ago, Miss Greer had offered free room and board to Sara Kaufman, one of Allie's best friends, in return for minor repair work and painting. Sara, on her own for the first time, had jumped at the chance. She'd lived there ever since.

But Sara wasn't here now. She'd taken off a few weeks ago, as she was prone to do.

Cooper Remington's beautiful silver BMW was parked in the street in front of the B and B. Pretentious creep. Another car, a flashy red Corvette, was parked across the street. Not a lawyer car. She wondered who carried the keys to that one in his pocket.

Realizing she was wasting time, she turned off the motor of her own car and got out. If she was lucky she would catch Cooper here, and she could plead her case. She took a deep breath and ordered herself to keep her temper firmly leashed. Flying off the handle wouldn't serve her purposes.

"Allie. How nice to see you," Miss Greer said pleasantly.

Allie folded her in a hug. At first the old woman was stiff as a plank, but Allie held on to her until she softened slightly and returned the hug, sort of. "It's nice to see you, too, Miss Greer. How's business?"

"It was a little slow, with Sara gone and the last of the snowbirds checking out yesterday. But these New Yorkers are filling in and the tourists are almost upon us."

"Is Mr. Remington here?" she asked politely.

"Which one?"

"Any of them." Maybe she wouldn't have to talk to Cooper directly.

"Mr. Cooper is in the dining room, working on a computer no bigger than a slice of bread. On a lovely day like this!"

Probably drafting eviction notices to serve on women and children somewhere. Lawyers just loved paperwork.

"I'll only keep him for a minute." A minute was all it would take to state her case and find out whether Cooper was a sensible sort or a complete jerk. She would put her money on the latter, if she'd had any money left to put.

She saw him before he saw her. He sat at the dining-room table, which he'd covered with stacks of paper and file folders. His slim laptop was open in front of him, and he was tapping furiously on it, his brow furrowed in concentration.

He certainly wasn't hard on the eyes. His hair was shorter than she normally liked, but it was a beautiful, deep-brown color. He had a lean face with movie-star cheekbones, a longish but straight nose, and a mouth that suggested to her all kinds of things she shouldn't think about in this context. His eyebrows were straight, dramatic slashes over eyes that she already knew were a deep, improbable shade of blue.

She tried to picture him relaxed in a deck chair wearing Hawaiian shorts and holding an umbrella drink.

Didn't work.

She cleared her throat. "Mr. Remington."

He looked up, obviously surprised. "Ms. Bateman. I didn't expect to see you here. If this is about our dispute, it would be wiser to communicate through your attorney."

"I have an appointment with my lawyer tomorrow, but he's unavailable today and there is a matter of some urgency I'd like to discuss." Nice. Be nice.

His gaze flickered behind her to the doorway. "Perhaps we should step outside."

"If you're worried about Miss Greer, don't be. She doesn't eavesdrop, and she would never repeat anything she inadvertently overheard."

"And you know this…how?"

"I've known the woman since I was in diapers, that's how."

"Still, I could use the fresh air."

Fine by her. Cooper led the way to the front door, opening it and holding it politely for her to go first. She got a whiff of his scent as she passed through the door, something refreshing and citrusy. Hmph. Did he think good manners and designer aftershave would impress her? But she took a nice deep breath just the same.

As soon as they were on the front porch with the door closed, she turned toward him. "Why did you request that injunction?"

He looked taken aback by her direct approach, but she didn't believe in mincing words.

Apparently he didn't, either. "You're a flight risk. You're about to lose a valuable asset, and you have no close ties in the area. You could—"

"No close ties?" She couldn't let that one pass. "I've lived in this town my whole life. I have dozens of close friends. Oh, but I guess friendship doesn't hold any weight in your world. Only blood ties." Blood ties who hadn't shown Johnny a speck of consideration when he was alive.

"Let's walk." Without waiting for her consent, he descended the porch steps to the brick walkway, giving her a nice view of his backside in those perfectly tailored khakis. What a waste, putting buns like that on a stiff-necked lawyer.

She followed, then took up beside him, matching his long strides. The way he strode along the street, oblivious to his surroundings, didn't surprise her. Like he wanted to clock in a few miles before lunch. Health-club mentality, typical of people whose jobs didn't require any physical exertion.

"Even if I could trust you," he said with arrogant confidence she would keep up with him, "there's always the chance something could happen to the boat while you're out—a storm, a wreck."

"That's hardly likely," she countered. "I'm an excellent sailor and I know the currents and the hazards as well as I know every splinter on the *Dragonfly*'s decks. The boat is fully insured. And I've never tried to cheat anyone in my life."

But Cooper didn't know her, so of course he would be suspicious that she would try to rip him off somehow. Lawyers believed everyone was trying to rip them off because *they* were trying to rip off everyone else.

"I am fully confident justice will prevail," she continued, "and I will keep my boat. You've checked by now and discovered that Johnny's will was properly filed and probated just as I said."

"It was a handwritten will."

"Which is called a holographic will," she retorted, "and you know as well as I do it's perfectly legal. But in case I'm wrong…what are you planning to do with Johnny's boat, if you get it?"

He answered without hesitation. "My cousins and I are going to continue to run the fishing charter service."

"Excuse me?" She laughed. She laughed until tears streamed from her eyes. Maybe her tears bordered on hysteria, but she honestly couldn't help it. The idea of these button-down Remington cousins running a fishing boat was ludicrous.

She had to stop and lean against a fence until she had herself under control. Cooper paused, arms folded, feet planted. Obviously he wasn't amused.

"Just what do you know about fishing?" she asked, wiping away her tears.

"You might be surprised. I worked on the *Dragonfly* when I was a teenager. I'm sure we have a lot to learn, but—"

"The first thing you ought to learn is that Remington Charters' most valuable asset is its reputation. Seventy percent of my business is repeat customers. You shut down the boat, force me to cancel cruises and send customers elsewhere, it could take years to undo the damage."

"I didn't think—"

"No, you didn't." She was on a roll now. "The business has bills to pay. You think docking a boat at the Port Clara Marina is cheap? You think my creditors will ever do business with you if your actions force me to stiff them?"

"Look, I have to protect my assets. But I've been thinking about things. In fact, I was working on a little proposition before you arrived."

Her hackles rose. What new trick had he come up with? "The boat is my asset, and what kind of proposition?"

"My cousins and I have discussed it, and we're prepared to offer you a generous cash settlement to quit your claim to the boat."

Oh, brother. "No."

He blinked a couple of times. "You haven't even heard how much."

"Doesn't matter. I would never willingly give up my boat. Johnny trusted me to take over for him and I'm not letting him down. I love fishing, I've been doing it since I was born and I'm good at it."

He stared at her until the eye contact became uncomfortable, but she refused to look away first. If he was seeking some outward sign of duplicity on her part, he wasn't going to get it.

"Then I'm sorry. The injunction stands."

"What could I do to change your mind?" She could hear the desperation creeping into her voice. "What if I brought a neutral party on board to keep tabs on me? Or…or…" The gears in her brain turned. She had an even better idea. Why hadn't she thought of this before?

He looked at her like she was crazy, but she knew she was on to something. "No, listen," she said excitedly. "This will work. You get that injunction lifted, let me continue with the charters, and any time the boat leaves port, you or one of your cousins can be on board. You said yourself that you'll need training—and I won't charge you for that. We can even split the proceeds." Half the income would be better than none. At least she could pay something to the most immediate of her creditors.

To her surprise, he actually seemed to think it over. Probably trying to work the angles, figure out how he could turn her idea to his benefit.

"A fifty-fifty split?"

"After expenses, of course. You can draw up the contract if you like." Of course he would want a contract. But if she could avoid canceling any trips, she would do it.

"I could reacquaint myself with the business that way," he said, thinking out loud.

"Exactly. See, a win-win situation. I know you lawyers generally prefer a win-lose option, but even you can see this is a sensible choice for us both." Especially if she could find a way to convince Cooper he didn't really want to run a fishing charter, that it wasn't the glamorous margarita party he thought it was.

Suddenly he smiled, and his face transformed. Her heart gave a little lurch. Oh, Lord, he was ten times more good-looking when he smiled.

"I guess that would make us partners," he said with an un-expected twinkle in his eye that made Allie's stomach swoop.

Maybe she should have thought this over first.

# Chapter Three

Cooper was surprised at how swiftly he'd agreed to Allie's counter-proposal. At Remington Industries he was known for taking a hard line, showing no mercy. No one would ever have accused him of being soft.

But before he could even think through all the ramifications or at least discuss matters with Reece and Max, he'd said okay. Maybe it was because he was itching to get back on board the *Dragonfly*; maybe it was the way Allie's chin had wobbled. But somehow he'd quickly convinced himself her idea had merit.

*Partners?* Where had that come from?

"I have to get back to the boat," Allie said. "I've got customers arriving in about thirty minutes. You call off the judge and draw up whatever papers you feel are necessary, but we depart at ten-thirty sharp. And, Cooper, you might want to change into shorts and deck shoes and…I don't know, maybe a shirt with some color in it? The clients expect Jimmy Buffet, not Warren Buffet."

Without giving him a chance to sputter any reply, she turned and jogged down the sidewalk to where she'd parked her old car. If she hadn't departed so abruptly, he'd have told her the wheels of justice don't turn that quickly. He couldn't simply undo the injunction and produce a contract out of thin air.

But surely no one would try to stop her from sailing, particularly if he, the complainant, were there to reassure any trigger-happy law-enforcement types that it was okay. As for the contract, he could draw it up tonight, provided Reece and Max agreed. Allie had actually made some good points about protecting the Remington Charters reputation by not canceling any excursions or turning away loyal customers, and Reece would approve of employing their asset to produce income, rather than letting it lie idle.

Cooper could use the sailing experience while they waited to take full ownership.

Surely his cousins would see the sense in such an argument.

But there was no time to worry about that now. He had to dig through his suitcase and come up with something that made him look less like a corporate lawyer and more like a happy-go-lucky beach bum.

At precisely 10:25, Cooper pulled his rental car into the marina parking lot and hurried to the *Dragonfly*'s slip. He wasn't worried that Allie would sail without him. But he didn't want to delay the cruise and have his customers believe their captain was a slow-moving slacker.

Yeah, Captain Cooper Remington. He liked that. And the customers would like it, too, having a man in charge. Not that he didn't believe Allie was competent. But she wasn't very big, probably not real strong, and fishing was a manly sport. If he were paying a bundle for a fishing charter, he would want someone who looked like he knew what he was doing to be giving advice.

He would avoid mentioning the word *captain* in front of Allie, though. First he would ease her into the idea that he was the one in charge.

As he approached the slip, he saw a group of men in shorts and golf shirts on deck. Some were milling around, others had already found deck chairs. Given their pale complexions, he guessed they were corporate execs on vacation.

Poor stiffs. He felt a bit smug, knowing he'd escaped the hallowed halls of corporate America to live his dream.

These were guys he understood.

"Good morning," he greeted them. "I'm Cooper Remington, your c—" He stopped himself just in time. "Your co-host. What's it going to be today, black drum? Maybe some Spanish mackerel?"

"Wrong season for mackerel," the oldest man in the group said, coming forward to peer critically at Cooper. "Allie says snapper are running thick in the bay. Remington, you said?"

"Yes, sir," Cooper responded, a tad less sure of himself now. Of course, mackerel season was later in the summer. He knew that. He thrust out his hand. "I'm the new owner of Remington Charters. Johnny was my uncle."

"Wait a minute," the older man said, holding up one finger. "Are you the nephew who puked on my fish?"

Cooper winced inwardly. A very long-time client, apparently. No wonder Allie hadn't wanted to disappoint him. "That was my cousin, Reece. I'm the one who cleaned the fish afterward." He'd been the only one capable. Reece couldn't stand to look at fish guts, and Max had been too young—and too easily distracted—to be trusted with a sharp knife.

"Well, okay then," the man said, backing off. "I'm sorry

for your loss. Johnny was a heckuva boat captain. I under-stood his gal was taking over."

"We have some legal technicalities to work through," Cooper said smoothly, "but for now she's helping me out. Can I get anyone a beverage?"

"Allie already showed us to the coffee," another of the men said. He had a thick Texas drawl, and Cooper already didn't like the way he said Allie's name or the sly smile that briefly crossed his face.

Allie shouldn't be running this business by herself. Captaining a boat the size of the *Dragonfly* was no easy task. Uncle Johnny had said that often enough. Storms, rocks and reefs, other boats piloted by people who didn't know what they were doing—hazards were everywhere, just waiting to waylay an inexperienced sailor. And then there were the predators—the two-legged variety. Allie's reaction to him and his cousins during their first encounter meant that she was at least aware of the threat.

But did she have any way to deal with it? Did she really have a gun, or was that a bluff? Would she even know how to shoot a firearm?

"We'll be under way soon," Cooper said. Soon as he found Allie and let her know he was on board and they could get started.

He went below, getting a first impression. The decor hadn't changed much in fifteen years. Still those same nautical-themed curtains at the windows; still the same blue carpeting. Everything was just more faded now. It did look as if someone had given the place a fresh coat of paint in recent history, and the seating area in the salon had new upholstery.

"Allie?"

"Down here."

That was when he spotted the open hatch. She was in the bowels of the boat. Cooper remembered that Johnny had spent a lot of time messing with the temperamental engines, which hadn't been new even back then.

Cooper moved closer, until he could see Allie, a wrench in her hand, a smear of grease across her face.

"Engine two won't start. You know anything about diesel engines?"

"Um, no." This wasn't good. His first time on a Remington Charters cruise as the owner, and the boat can't leave the dock? Made him look like an idiot. "I can call a mechanic."

"Only if you can pay for it out of your pocket. I can't use the operating account."

"We have to call—"

"Just give me a few more minutes," she said crossly. "I think I know what the problem is. Are the troops growing restless?"

"They seemed happy enough when I greeted them. And why is there no money in the operating account?" He couldn't help the sharp note of suspicion in his question. Just because Allie had big green eyes and a really cute turned-up nose was no reason to believe she was too innocent to wipe out the company coffers. She could have done it Friday, after kicking Cooper and his cousins off the boat.

She looked at him as if he were the stupidest person in the world. "You froze the account."

"Right." He'd forgotten about that.

"But even if you hadn't, the business isn't exactly rolling in money. I had to make some very expensive repairs to the engines a couple of weeks ago, repairs which were supposed to prevent *this*—" she pointed an accusing finger at the ailing engine "—from happening. The insurance rates have gone up again. Then there's the price of fuel and… Why am I telling you this? Just look at the damn books."

She leaned over the engine again, applying her wrench to a rusty bolt with no success. By propping one shapely leg against the boat's hull as leverage, she finally cracked the nut loose. She unscrewed it and lifted a metal plate, revealing a spaghetti bowl of multicolored wires.

"Ah-hah," she said with a note of triumph. "Just as I thought, another short. Would you look at this wire? It could have caused a fire. When I get hold of Mickey…" She busied herself yanking the charred wire from the spaghetti, then reached into a tool box for a length of replacement wire. She deftly stripped the rubber casing off the ends and reconnected…whatever it was that had become disconnected.

"Who's Mickey?" Cooper asked.

"Worst mechanic in Port Clara, that's who. Could you go turn the ignition and see if the thing starts?"

"Won't it just short out again?"

"Maybe. But I have lots of wire. I'll just have to jerry-rig it well enough to get through the day. Then I'll call Mickey and have him fix it right this time."

"Shouldn't you call someone else?"

She pointed the wrench at him. "Ignition? Please?"

Cooper didn't like being ordered around. But the fact was, she obviously knew more about boat engines than him. If there was one thing corporate law had taught him, it was that knowledge is power.

He would have to learn. Meanwhile, maybe allowing Allie to stick around awhile—just till he got his sea legs—

wasn't such a bad idea. And speaking of legs, he needed to stop looking at hers, even if she insisted on showing them off in those Daisy Dukes.

He was baffled by the fact she'd refused to even entertain a settlement. She was going to lose everything.

He climbed up to the bridge. A set of well-worn keys dangled from the ignition. He turned the key, and both engines sputtered to life. He whispered a prayer of thanks that he didn't have to disappoint loyal customers.

As he took the ship's wheel in his hands, a wave of nostalgia washed over Cooper. One of the proudest moments in his youth had come when Uncle Johnny let him drive this boat for the first time. He'd secretly pretended to be a pirate, scanning the murky waters for telltale turbulence that meant an obstacle below the surface—then scanning the horizon for merchant ships to plunder.

He heard a noise behind him and turned. Allie had joined him at the bridge, a pleased smile on her face. It was the first time he'd seen her smile, and even his jaded, suspicious heart wasn't immune to the effects.

Oh, she was a heartbreaker, all right. Uncle Johnny, an aging, alcoholic widower, must have been putty in her hands.

"Do you know how to cast off?" she asked.

"You can do that," he said smoothly, gripping the wheel more tightly. "My place is here."

"Like hell. Get off my bridge."

"Our bridge. We're partners, remember?"

"Have you ever piloted a boat in your life?"

"Yes. Uncle Johnny taught me."

"How long ago?"

All right, so it had been more than twenty years ago. "It's like riding a bicycle."

"Have you even looked at a nautical chart in the last ten years? Sandbars have moved. Reefs have changed. So if you even remember where all the hazards were umpteen years ago, they're different now. We have a new sonar system since you were here. Do you know how to use it?"

She gave him a derisive up-and-down visual exam, taking in his choice of sailing clothes, no doubt. Khaki shorts, a golf shirt and Top Sider moccasins with white soles—perfectly sensible, weekend-casual clothing—in fact, very similar to what the passengers wore. But he felt almost too formal. She wore only those faded cutoffs and a white tank shirt with an embroidered Remington Charters logo over her left breast. And a nice breast it was.

She also had the tanned skin and gold sun streaks in her hair to prove her authenticity.

A wave of heat washed over him. Funny, he'd never found the outdoorsy girls to be his type before. Most of the women he'd dated were professionals—with a few idle heiresses thrown in. But even though Allie was out to fleece him, he found her lack of pretense refreshing and appealing. No makeup, no long lacquered nails, no five-hundred-dollar shoes or salon highlights. Just five-foot-three of pure woman.

Gradually he loosened his grip on the wheel. He hated to admit it, but she was right. He was acting like a macho jerk.

"Do you know where to find snapper?" she asked.

He backed away from the controls, holding his hands out in a gesture of surrender. "Okay, fine. Today you're the captain and I'm the first mate. But tomorrow we'll trade." He would watch everything she did and reassure himself he was perfectly capable. How hard could it be?

ALLIE STEAMED AS SHE GUIDED the *Dragonfly* out of its slip and across the no-wake area around the marina. Did Cooper Remington honestly think he could just waltz in here and start running charter excursions on childhood memories?

It was tempting to let him have the *Dragonfly*. Let him sink the business, if not the boat, before his first season closed.

But she couldn't walk away. Everything she had, everything she'd built over the years, was tied up in this business. All the money she'd saved to buy her own boat, she'd sunk into the *Dragonfly* to keep her afloat since Johnny's illness set in. She couldn't face starting from scratch.

She could probably get a job with one of the other charter services. Yeah, they were all competitors, but friendly ones. Everybody in Port Clara—and up and down the Texas coast, for that matter—knew she had the experience, not to mention an uncanny sixth sense for finding the fish. Her boat might be humble, but her customers always left with full coolers.

Once she got into open water she set a course for the most likely place to find schools of snapper. It would take more than an hour to get there. During that time she needed to make sure all the men had the correct equipment and bait, and she had to serve them up a snack.

This group was easy. They'd all fished with her before and they knew their stuff. Mr. Cox, who'd been fishing for forty years—most of those with Johnny—could answer any questions. Her only real challenge was to avoid Mr. Nelson's roaming hands.

She looked down at the deck and spotted Cooper. He'd found a deck chair and a soft drink and was in an animated conversation with one of the passengers. She was going to have to watch him every minute—the guy was used to being waited on, not the other way around. And God knew what he was telling her customers.

"Cooper!" she called down. "Come take over the helm." All he had to do was go in a straight line and avoid hitting any other boats. Surely he could handle that.

He looked up at her and grinned. "Aye-aye, cap'n."

Once she had him safely ensconced in the captain's chair, she set to work with the rods and reels, making sure each man had equipment he was happy with, untangling line, figuring out who would be positioned where.

"Is it true, what that Remington boy said?" Mr. Cox asked in a low voice. "Is he taking over the business?"

"He's going to try." Allie made it sound like she wasn't concerned. "Johnny's family isn't happy about the status quo, and Cooper is going to try to break the will."

"Think he can do it?"

"The Remingtons have large coffers of discretionary cash to fight a legal battle. Obviously I don't. So we'll have to see."

"That hardly seems fair."

Allie patted Mr. Cox on the arm. "Life's never fair." So far, that had been her experience. But she kept thinking that sooner or later she'd get an even shake. She'd already had her father's boat stolen out from under her by her conniving uncle. She deserved a break.

"I just want you to know," Mr. Cox said, "that I'll take my business wherever you land. You know your stuff."

His loyalty touched her. She had so many good friends in Port Clara, but she also knew people from all over the country and the world. Johnny's customers had hailed from as far away as Vancouver and Buffalo—even Japan. Many of them had booked again this season, even after learning of Johnny's death. They were willing to give her a try. If all of them were as loyal as Mr. Cox, she could bring a valuable client list to any other boat she signed on with.

But that thought didn't cheer her much. She loved *this* boat. She'd put so much care into it—painting, sewing new cushion covers for the salon, scrubbing the hull. She'd even designed the Remington Charters logo, with Jane's help.

All so the rich Remington boys could trash it.

Okay, she didn't know for sure they would, but it wasn't their lifeblood or they wouldn't have spent all those years in New York pursuing landlocked jobs. This was a lark for them. If they sank the boat or trashed the business, they would just move on to their next entertainment.

Like her uncle had, after he'd trashed her father's business. Last she knew the *Ginnie,* named after her mother, was in Key West.

Allie shook off her nostalgia. She had snacks to put out—cold cuts and bread for sandwiches, apple and orange wedges, potato chips and pretzels.

Once she had the food squared away she checked on Cooper. She stood at the top of the ladder, watching him without his notice. Already he looked less buttoned-up, more relaxed. With the wind ruffling his short hair and the sun on his face, he was more handsome than ever. But it was the expression on his face that stopped her, made her reconsider.

He looked blissed out. Like he'd never been so happy. Obviously he did love sailing, even if he'd been away for a while. For the first time she could see a family resemblance between Cooper and his uncle.

She felt her heart softening toward him even as other parts of her sprang to life.

*No.* Cooper was the enemy. He was out to steal her

dreams, and she had best remember that—even if, right this moment, she wanted nothing more than to stand beside him at the wheel, put her hands on his sun-warmed shirt, and share with him the giddy joy of sailing on the high seas.

COOPER'S FIRST CHARTER CRUISE was a success. As he said goodbye to the passengers, who lugged coolers bulging with fish they'd caught, he felt an overwhelming sense of well-being.

Coming here to claim his inheritance had been the right decision. He and Max could run the boat. Maybe they could hire Allie to handle refreshments. But even as that possibility crossed his mind, he knew it would never happen. Allie was used to running the show. She wouldn't settle for taking a backseat.

Anyway, they needed someone who could prepare gourmet meals in a small galley. Sandwiches and chips were fine, but if they wanted to attract an upscale clientele and charge more money, they had to upgrade.

The *Dragonfly* wouldn't be the same without Allie, he caught himself thinking. In only one day he'd gotten used to seeing her running all over the boat, surefooted as a monkey, handling several tasks at once. She would fetch drinks for the passengers, re-bait a hook, and check on the engine to make sure it hadn't caught fire all in the span of a minute or two.

She was good. He hated to admit it, but she was. He never would have found the fish. But she would analyze the sonar, gaze at the water, then—no kidding—sniff the air. A few minutes later, there would be a school of snapper. Watching her was like sipping good Scotch.

The sight of her rounded bottom in those tight denim

shorts had provided its own entertainment. Much as he enjoyed the sight, he ought to talk to her about her uniform.

Harry Nelson hadn't been able to keep his ogling eyes off of her, either, and it wouldn't be good for business if Cooper had to punch out one of the passengers for taking liberties with his staff.

Allie worked side by side with him now, helping the happy, sunburned passengers with their gear. As soon as everyone else had disembarked, he turned to her and grinned, unable to help himself.

"We did it."

"Did you think we wouldn't?"

He shrugged. "I'm just saying we did good. Do we have people booked for tomorrow?"

"We have a ten o'clock, but normally the start time is much earlier." Tomorrow, however, she had to meet with her lawyer first thing.

"Guess I'll see you around nine, then." He turned, but she grabbed his arm.

"Whoa, whoa, whoa. Where do you think you're going? Just because the passengers are gone doesn't mean our workday is over. We have to clean and put away the equipment. Carry out the trash. Empty the holding tanks. Call Mickey about fixing the engine. Then we have to get ready for tomorrow. We have to lay in groceries, bait."

"Does it really take two people to—"

"Excuse me. Partners, remember? If you want half the profits, you gotta do half the work."

"I have obligations," he said. "Bank accounts to un-freeze. Injunctions to un-injunct. A contract to draft." Truthfully, he'd arranged for Reece to handle most of those tasks. But if he was going to captain this boat tomorrow, he had some studying to do. He supposed it wasn't fair to stick Allie with all the chores. But tomorrow he would be ready to pitch in.

"Tell you what. Tomorrow I'll do all the cleaning and shopping and whatever. You can have the evening off."

She raised one eyebrow. "Really?"

"Sure."

"Okay, deal."

He reached into his pocket, pulled out his money clip, and peeled off five hundred-dollar bills. "That should handle incidentals until you're able to access the business account."

Allie stared at the money with bulging eyes. "Do you always carry that kind of money around?"

"I like to be prepared. See you tomorrow."

He stepped off the boat, feeling really good about the day. He had pleasantly sore muscles from climbing up and down the ladder to the bridge, and his nose was sunburned.

His good mood lasted until he saw Reece striding toward him down the dock, looking ridiculously out of place in dress slacks, a starched white shirt and a tie. Why was he wearing a tie? No one down here wore ties unless they were getting married or going to a funeral.

"Where the hell have you been?" Reece demanded. "Why haven't you answered your phone?"

"Um, Reece, cell phones don't work out on the ocean. Is there a problem?"

"I'll say. Mark Gold called from Austin."

Gold was the legal researcher Cooper had hired to check into Allie's claims about a will. "What did he say?"

"He says there is a will. Handwritten, but properly witnessed, properly executed in every way. Went through probate without a hitch. It leaves the boat to one Allison Therese Bateman."

"We'll hire a forgery expert," Cooper said immediately. "The whole thing could be faked. Uncle Johnny wouldn't have cut us out."

"Apparently he did. I've talked to the lawyer here who filed it. His name is Arlen Caldwell. He was a personal friend of Johnny's. Says there is no question that Johnny wrote and signed the will."

"If that's true, we'll argue diminished mental capacity. And if that doesn't work, we'll prove Allie coerced him into writing a new will."

"Caldwell says Johnny was perfectly sane, and there's not a chance he was coerced."

"Damn it, Reece, I'm not letting her get away with this. That's our boat. She's not even distantly related. Say, wait a minute, how old is this Caldwell character?"

Reece shrugged. "I don't know, I didn't meet him. But on the phone he sounds like an old man."

"Bingo. Allie Bateman wrapped one old man around her little finger. Why not two?"

"You think she and Caldwell were in it together?"

"Why not?"

Reece appeared dubious. "Look, Coop, just because Heather did a number on you—"

"I told you before, do *not* bring Heather into this. She has nothing to do with the current situation."

"Of course she does. She snowed you. She snowed the whole family. She stole nearly a quarter million dollars—"

"I know what she did."

"And she got away with it. But that doesn't mean every woman in the world is a conniving siren out to fleece us.

We can fight Johnny's will, but it's going to cost us. Plenty. After seeing the boat, I'm not sure it's worth it."

"And after spending all day aboard the *Dragonfly,* I'm sure it is," Cooper countered. Piloting that boat, feeling the wind, smelling the tangy salt air, he'd felt more alive than he had in years. He was pretty sure Allie's presence on the boat had nothing to do with the high he'd felt all day. "I'll pay the legal fees from my own pocket if I have to, but I'm not giving up."

# Chapter Four

Allie finally got the boat squared away. Mickey had come over after hours and banged around on the engine for a while. When he was done, it didn't appear anything had changed. If anything, there were more wires added to the spaghetti bowl. But the scruffy mechanic swore Allie wouldn't have any more electrical shorts.

What were the chances of that being true?

After making a careful notation in the ledger book, she'd used Cooper's money to pay off Dino and buy groceries for the next day's excursions.

She was grateful for the cash, and she would repay him as soon as she had access to the money from today's charter. But she'd probably been a fool to make a side deal with Cooper Remington. She had her doubts he'd do all the post-cruise work tomorrow while she took the evening off. Would he even know what to do?

Though she had to get up early tomorrow—she was meeting Arlen at the crack of dawn—she was too restless to go to bed, so she locked up the boat and headed for Old Salt's. Johnny used to hang out there a lot, before he quit drinking. It was a friendly bar favored by the locals, and she imagined she would see a few familiar faces there.

If she lost the *Dragonfly,* at least she would still have her friends. No one could take them away from her.

"Hey, Allie!" The enthusiastic greeting came from Jimmy Pye, who captained the *Sallie Ann.* They often referred business back and forth. "Heard you found the snapper today."

"We pulled in a few," she said with a grin, slapping the crusty sailor on the back as she passed his table, where he was tipping some beers with his crew.

"How's it goin', Allie?" another sailor asked. He was a skinny man she knew only as Paco who had crewed for several different boats over the years.

She couldn't honestly answer that things were going great, but she had no intention of airing her problems in a public place. "Things are goin'," she said noncommittally.

Several others greeted her with a friendly wave or a nod. They were a close-knit group, the sailors and boat owners of Port Clara. By now, news of the injunction had spread, but no one mentioned it. They knew she would talk about it if she wanted to.

She slid onto a bar stool and was surprised to see her friend Sara behind the bar, mixing drinks.

"Hey, *que pasa, chica?*" Sara grinned, her huge chandelier earrings forming a glittering halo. Sara was a spot of sunshine wherever she went. She liked to wear Mexican cotton shirts embroidered with bright colors, and swirly skirts that often clashed. Today she'd twisted her long, brown hair into a careless knot on top of her head, stuck through with a pencil.

"When did you come back?" Allie asked as her friend

poured her a Corona draft without asking. "I thought you'd be gone at least a couple more weeks."

Sara shrugged as she set the frosty mug in front of Allie along with a bowl of lime wedges. "Got tired of L.A. Too expensive, too plastic…and the art-house movie I was supposed to work on turned out to be more porn than art. Like they really needed a set designer? I told 'em to buy a king-size bed and some gauze, and I walked."

That was Sara. Easy come, easy go.

"Anyway, I got a little homesick," she admitted.

"You? Homesick?"

"Well, okay, I heard three very good-looking, rich and highly eligible bachelors were staying at the B and B, and my curiosity got the better of me."

Allie squeezed some lime juice into her beer. "So you heard."

Sara frowned. "Yeah. Miss Greer called me. Actually, I think she was just looking for an excuse to check up on me. Sounds like you got some real trouble on your hands, doll. What's the scoop?"

"Ugh. I'll fill you in sometime, but not tonight. Tonight I just want to forget those Remington cousins exist."

"Then you came to the wrong place." Sara's gaze slid to the left, and Allie suppressed a gasp. There they were, at a table not twenty feet away. They each had a bottle of some fancy designer beer, and they had their heads together, poring over a bunch of papers.

"I'll have to agree with Miss Greer," Sara said. "Those Remington boys are a nice-looking lot—especially the one with the glasses. He's cute."

Allie frowned and squinted at them. "You think so?" Cooper was the one whose looks made her mouth go dry.

"Mmm-mmm. Don't you want to go and just muss up that neatly combed hair?"

"Sara. Don't forget, those guys are trying to take away my boat. I can't afford to let up my guard for one minute, and that means no hair mussing."

Sara cocked her head to one side. "I don't know, hon, but I think you could do better making friends, rather than seeing them as the enemy."

"*You* go make friends, then," Allie huffed. "Find out what they're talking about."

"I think maybe I will." Sara moved to the adjacent side of the square bar area, near the Remingtons' table, while Allie nursed her beer and angled her body away from the men. The bar was pretty crowded, so they probably wouldn't see her.

A reporter from the *Port Clara Clarion* stopped by to chat, casually milking Allie for information about the *Dragonfly*'s disputed ownership, but Allie gave the woman as little as possible. She kept watch on the Remingtons from the corner of her eye.

At least, she thought she'd kept watch. But when a pair of strong hands gripped her shoulders from behind, she nearly came off her bar stool.

"Allie!" Cooper said in a jovial greeting, as if they were old friends. "Why don't you join us at our table? I'll buy you a drink."

His hands on her, so casually, should have been repugnant. But to her utter disgust, she found his touch sparked something deep inside her, something female responding to his masculinity.

"I don't think so," she said coolly.

"Aw, come on." He released her and slid onto the bar

stool next to her. "We had a great time today. Don't let our legal dispute color everything black."

She gave him her most penetrating stare. "You call it a legal dispute. I call it you trying to take away my livelihood."

The easy smile fled his face. She wished he wasn't so darn good-looking. It would be easier to hold on to her righteous indignation if he didn't tickle her hormones.

"I did offer you a cash settlement," he reminded her. "But you wouldn't even listen. Litigation is expensive."

She'd been wondering if she was crazy not to at least listen to his offer. If it was generous enough, she could start over, maybe buy an interest in another boat.

She could even compete with the Remingtons.

But selling out didn't sit well with her. Johnny had trusted *her* to take care of his boat and his business after he was gone. He'd obviously not been on good terms with his family, and he wouldn't want them to have the *Dragonfly* or Remington Charters.

"I know litigation is expensive."

He raised an eyebrow in feigned surprise. "Oh? You've been sued before, perhaps? Are property disputes a pattern with you?"

"I'm not some black widow preying on old men, if that's what you think. But I have had dealings with lawyers."

Allie's father had died when she was sixteen. He'd been a charter fisherman, too—friends with Johnny, in fact. He'd left everything to Allie in his will, but her attorney-uncle was the executor of the estate until she reached majority. Within eighteen months he'd bankrupted the business. She'd tried to get legal help when she realized what was happening, but no lawyer would take her case because she didn't have any money.

She didn't, however, think her past legal problems were any of Cooper's business. He would use any little tidbit he picked up from her to defeat her. He would twist her words until she came out sounding like an opportunist who went around inheriting boats as a hobby.

"We're not all jerks," Cooper pointed out.

"Prove it."

"It's not as if the boat means nothing to me." He tried again. "I spent summers with Uncle Johnny when I was younger—Reece and Max, too. They're the happiest memories we have. Is it wrong for us to want to reclaim those happy times? Especially when I know Johnny always intended for us to inherit his boat someday. He used to tell us that all the time."

Oh, he was good. She'd give him that. If a jury heard their case—and knowing what she so far knew of Cooper, he would demand a jury hearing—they would be whipping out their handkerchiefs before he was through with them.

"Maybe once upon a time he did intend to leave you the boat. But that was before you went years without visiting, without calling. Before you left him to die here alone, with only his employee by his bedside."

"His employee?" Another raised eyebrow.

"His employee and his dear friend, and *nothing more*."

"You lived together on the boat. Am I supposed to believe—"

"Yes, that's exactly what you're supposed to believe. You've clearly been asking around, but you won't find a single person in this town who will claim Johnny and I were romantically involved. Not anyone who knew us, anyway."

He shrugged. "Pity for you. If you could claim status as his common-law wife, your chances in court would go up."

She slapped some money on the bar, gave him one more hard look, and left. She wasn't going to dignify his observation with a response.

She didn't need to resort to legal tricks. The law was on her side.

"Shot you down, did she?" Max said as Cooper reclaimed his chair at their table. Even with a black eye, Max was still a chick magnet. He'd made up some ridiculous story about fighting off a mugger, and he'd already secured dates with two different women.

Cooper gathered up the papers they'd been working on, just some brainstorming on ways to market the charter service once ownership was established. "Allie's a tough cookie. Says she's dealt with lawyers before. I'll put Mark Gold to work finding out exactly what sort of litigation she's been involved in."

He caught Reece and Max sharing a look.

"What?"

"Nothing," Reece said, draining the last of his Coke.

"You guys think I'm going too far?"

"Duh." Max threw a few bills on the table for their waitress. "Why don't we just let the judge sort it out? If Uncle Johnny really wanted to give his girlfriend a boat, who are we to say no?"

"She wasn't his girlfriend." Cooper was surprised at how quickly he argued that point. But he did believe Allie about that one thing. No one in town had supported his theory that Allie and Johnny were lovers.

Max shrugged. "Whatever."

Why didn't his cousins get it? Maybe not every woman was out to fleece the male population, but he'd seen enough of the world to know that you should never trust one without proof she was honest.

Even his own mother made no bones about the fact that she'd married his father more for security than love, though the marriage must have worked on some level, because they were still together and seemed happy, at least outwardly.

"Women in my day didn't have the choices available to men," she'd explained. "I had to marry wealth. I grew up with it, and I wasn't keen to give it up. Fortunately your father was willing to keep me in the manner to which I'd become accustomed."

Cooper had never been sure if she was joking or not.

If Johnny's honest intention was to renege on his promise to his nephews and cut them out of his will, Cooper was willing to honor his uncle's wishes. But he considered it his responsibility to be absolutely sure they weren't all being hoodwinked.

ARLEN CALDWELL WAS CLOSE to eighty years old, but his mind was as sharp as any twenty-year-old's. Unfortunately his eyes weren't; he inspected his photocopy of Johnny's will with a magnifying glass.

He and Allie were seated in his office, which was small and unassuming. The carpeting had a worn track where the attorney no doubt paced as he worked out exactly how he would help his clients to prevail. His leather desk chair was scuffed at the corners, and he still used a wooden file cabinet.

But everything was neat and scrupulously clean, thanks to his longtime secretary, Janice, who didn't mind running a dust cloth over the furniture now and then.

Arlen was a good lawyer, and his age was actually a

point in his favor. Sometimes opposing attorneys underestimated him, falling for his doddering-old-fool act.

"It's all just as I remember it," he said after ten minutes of close scrutiny. "It's entirely proper. So long as the date on this will supersedes the other, and no one can prove Johnny was coerced or incompetent, this will stands."

Allie wasn't entirely relieved. "Coerced or incompetent" left a lot of wiggle room.

"'Course, we'll want a sworn statement from Jane Simone that she did witness Johnny signing the will and that he wasn't drunk or crazy. Is she from around here?"

"She lives in Houston, but I'm sure she won't mind making a statement. She's a good friend. She would even come down here and testify in person, I'm sure. She just needs to know when so she can make arrangements for childcare and such."

Jane had an adorable little girl named Kaylee. Her husband couldn't be counted on to baby-sit—he was a workaholic. Sometimes she wondered why he'd bought the beautiful cabin cruiser, because he seldom sailed it. Jane usually came down just with Kaylee.

"Johnny wasn't back on the bottle, was he?" Arlen asked.

"No, sir, absolutely not. I hadn't seen him drink a drop this century."

"What about the cancer drugs? The pain meds? Did they make him groggy or loopy?"

"Some. But he didn't like that, so he usually only took one pain pill right before bed so he could sleep. I can assure you he was awake and alert the day he wrote his will, and Jane will back me up."

"I have to ask you this, Allie, but whose idea was it that he write a new will?"

"It was his," she answered without hesitation. "I'd put

a lot of my own money into upkeep of the *Dragonfly,* and he was worried that I'd lose everything when he died. He wanted to protect me. He said he was estranged from his family and they didn't care anything about an old boat."

"Oh. You have financial records, I hope."

"Absolutely. I make detailed notes about every transaction having to do with the business. I brought copies." She placed the manila envelope she'd brought with her on his desk.

He patted her hand in a grandfatherly gesture. "Don't you worry. We'll send those Yankees back to New York with their tails between their legs."

"I hope you're right." She stood up. "How much do you reckon this will cost me?"

"Well, let's see…court fees, photocopies, parking—a hundred dollars, give or take."

"What about your fee?"

"This one's on me, kiddo. Johnny would haunt me from the grave if I let those big-city boys push you around."

ALLIE FELT A LITTLE BETTER about things, until she returned to the *Dragonfly* and found Cooper standing on the dock with Pete Dodson, inspecting the boat's hull. Now what was he doing hanging around with that scalawag?

"Oh, good morning, Allie," Cooper said when he saw her approaching. "Where've you been so bright and early?"

"Seeing my lawyer," she said pointedly.

"Hey, Allie," Pete said. "Your new partner here's hired me to do some paintin'. 'Bout time, too. The old girl is lookin' pretty shabby."

"Oh, really?" She stared daggers at Cooper. "Mr. Remington, might I have a word with you in private?" She turned without waiting for his agreement, unlocked the hatch, and went below.

Cooper followed, looking bewildered. "Something wrong?"

She poured herself some cold coffee and stuck it in the microwave. "Yes, as a matter of fact. Number one, there's no money in the budget for painting. Number two, if there was money, we would do it in the winter, not right when the tourist season is upon us. Number three, *if* it was winter, and if we had money in the budget to paint, we would not hire Pete."

"What's wrong with Pete? He says he'll give us the best price."

"He'll give us a quote, and then he'll nickel-and-dime us to death, or he'll walk off and leave the job half done because someone else has offered him a more lucrative job. Plus, he's the slowest painter in all of Texas."

"Well, hell, Allie. I thought I was doing a good thing. The boys and I were brainstorming ways to bring in more customers and charge them more. Anyway, I was just talking to Pete. I haven't actually hired him. I was going to talk to several boat painters. And I was going to pay for it."

"And when the judge awards me ownership of this boat, how would I pay you back?"

Cooper shrugged. "Guess I'd take you to court and file a lien on the boat till you paid—come on, Allie," he said when she shrieked, "I'm not serious. I wouldn't ask for the money back."

"I'm supposed to trust you on this? If our positions were reversed, would you trust me?"

Ah. She could see she had him there. He looked slightly guilty, but only for a moment. "Just how bad are the Remington Charters finances?"

"Bad enough. I didn't run any trips those last few weeks. After Johnny died…" she was embarrassed that her voice cracked "…it took a while for me to start booking charters again, and I'm still not up to speed, though business is picking up. I've been living hand-to-mouth, juggling the bills, paying only the most urgent."

His mouth thinned to a tight crease. "Can we look at the books? Reece is a CPA. Maybe he can help."

"I've given my lawyer copies of everything pertinent, and I'm sure he'll send you copies."

"Everything pertinent?"

"Well, not every single page of the ledger, but receipts and copies of bills and what-not."

"Reece will want to see it all."

"The only thing that will help the finances is lots of paying customers—which we should have in the normal course of business. I expect I'll get caught up in a few weeks. But you're welcome to inspect the books—on the premises."

"Only one problem with that. Reece gets seasick."

"They make wonderful medicine for that these days." She took a long sip of her cold coffee. Blech. "We better go give the bad news to Pete that we aren't hiring him."

She could tell Cooper didn't like it that she'd made the decision. But hers was the name on the *Dragonfly*'s title.

At least for a while longer.

## Chapter Five

Allie got her second surprise when she stepped into the galley to prepare snacks for their 10:00 a.m. charter. A case of upscale beer now occupied the entire lower two shelves of her refrigerator. Either Cooper had a powerful thirst, or he planned on serving their guests alcohol.

She climbed the steps to the deck, where Cooper was wiping everything down with a sponge and a bucket of soapy water. He wasn't afraid of hard work, she'd give him that. Once he got a glimmering of how much work there was to do in preparation for each excursion, he'd jumped right in.

"Cooper!"

He looked up with a grin. "Yes, Allie?"

"Have you ever dealt with a bunch of drunks on a boat, armed with fishhooks? It's not pretty."

"I seem to remember Uncle Johnny serving drinks to the guests."

Yeah, Allie remembered that, too—and a few cruises where the captain was drunker than the passengers. At least she'd learned how to pilot the boat by then.

"It's too much for me to handle alone," she argued.

"My cousins and I have been doing some research. If we make high-quality cocktails available, we can charge a lot more. We can hire a college kid to tend bar—in fact, I talked to the bartender at Old Salt last night and she'd be willing to do it for a few bucks."

"Sara?" Allie would have a few words to say to her friend. "I don't want drunk passengers."

"I'll make sure that doesn't happen. You want to make a profit, don't you?"

She started to argue that she did make a profit. But with the current state of her finances, she couldn't make a good argument. "Fine. You handle it, though. And if somebody gets drunk and falls overboard, it's on your head."

Once they got that argument out of the way, the morning went more smoothly. Their passengers included two couples and their preteen kids. Children always made Allie a bit nervous, especially when their parents didn't control them. They usually required a great deal of one-on-one instruction. But this group was well-behaved. And to her surprise, Cooper handled the instruction part just fine.

Apparently he did know something about fishing.

When she brought out the platters of cold cuts for lunch, she saw that Cooper was patiently coaching the youngest member of their party, a ten-year-old girl, to pull in her first fish. It was a beautiful red snapper, quite a large one, and Allie held her breath as the girl struggled valiantly to get it into the boat.

A lot of men would simply have taken over for the small girl, but Cooper cheered on her efforts and offered advice when needed, stepping in only when the fish was out of the water.

"Nicely done, Brenna." Cooper had the fish safely in a net.

The little girl beamed, but then her smile faded. "Do I have to eat him? Or can I put him back in the ocean?"

Cooper looked at the fish thoughtfully. "He'd be good eating. But if you'd like to let him go, that's okay."

"Can I, Daddy?" she asked her father.

The girl's father looked pained—his mouth was probably already watering at the thought of grilled snapper for dinner tonight. But he nodded.

Allie couldn't help smiling as Cooper took the fish off the hook and wistfully threw it back in the water. But her smile fled as he stepped away from the family and peeled off his golf shirt, which had apparently gotten wet.

She nearly dropped her platter.

Holy cow, muscles like that ought to be outlawed. Maybe he'd built himself up at some pricey health club rather than with hard physical labor, but her hormones sure didn't know the difference. He had a bit of a farmer's tan—or rather, a golfer's tan. But a few more days on the boat with his shirt off, and he'd be smooth, golden brown all over.

She shivered at the thought.

Maybe she should get out more. The fact the thought of touching Cooper even crossed her mind felt like a betrayal to Johnny.

She passed a container of moist towelettes so everyone could wipe their hands before eating.

"What can I get everyone to drink?" Cooper asked. "We have all kinds of soft drinks, water and Sam Adams beer."

One of the men grinned. "Now you're talking. Bring all the adults a beer."

Hmm. She hated to admit it, but maybe Cooper was right.

They'd scarcely gotten the families disembarked when their afternoon passengers arrived, a group of young, testosterone-laden men. They were probably close to her age, and all of them as handsome as good breeding and lots of money could make them, but not a one of them flipped her switch, even when they flirted with her mercilessly.

"Heck, Allie," one of the men said when she turned him down for a date later that night. "One of the main reasons we picked your boat was because your picture's on the Web site."

But Cooper gave him a hard stare and he backed down.

By the time they were heading back to the harbor, the weather had turned. Threatening thunderheads had pushed in from the south, and the ocean was a bit rougher than it had been. It took all of Allie's concentration to keep the boat from bucking.

Cooper appeared at the bridge. "One of the passengers is seasick. Do we have some medicine we could give him?"

"Yes, but I can't hunt it down right now."

"I can take the bridge."

Allie's first instinct was to say *no way*. Piloting the boat in smooth waters was one thing, but in this chop?

Then again, Cooper had so far proved himself perfectly capable. He'd watched her navigate in and out of the harbor three times now; he was probably up to it, and the seas were smoothing out as they got into more protected water.

"Yeah, okay. Just be careful. The rocks we passed on our way out are hidden by high tide now."

"I remember."

She scampered down the ladder and below, where one of the men was indeed looking a bit green around the gills. She might regret serving the guys beer after all.

The instructions she gave all passengers with their reservation confirmation included a list of things they should bring with them, and that included seasick medicine, though she always kept some on hand. But she had to rummage around in a couple of cabinets before she found it.

She gave some to the green man, then headed back toward the bridge. She checked their position just before climbing the ladder.

Damn it, Cooper was heading straight for those rocks. She climbed as fast as she could, yelling as she did.

"Swing hard to port! You're gonna—"

A loud thump cut her off. Oh, God. They'd hit something.

By the time she reached the bridge he'd swung left, and the boat was chugging away from the hazard.

He turned over the wheel with a murmured "Sorry."

She resisted the urge to yell at him, because she'd done the same thing once when she was learning to pilot her father's boat. They'd probably only bumped a rock.

Anyway, she was the captain. She was responsible for what happened on this boat.

"The currents are tricky here," she explained. "And when the water's rough, the *Dragonfly* doesn't respond as quickly."

Cooper said nothing, but she could tell he felt bad.

"You want to take her in?" she asked, because she knew exactly what he felt like. And she remembered that after she'd nearly wrecked the *Ginnie,* she'd been terrified to take the wheel again. But her father had explained that it was like riding a bicycle. If you didn't get right back on after falling off, you might be scared of bikes the rest of your life.

"I'll watch you take her in," he said quietly. "Maybe I have more to learn than I thought."

Well, would miracles never cease? The man who'd stormed her boat acting like he knew everything had just admitted he didn't.

She ought to be glad he'd had a scare. Maybe he would realize running a charter service wasn't all fun and games and change his mind about his new direction in life.

But that wouldn't help, she realized. He would still try to take the *Dragonfly* away. Then he would sell her future to the highest bidder.

REECE WAS WAITING AT THE DOCK when they pulled in. Although the rain had come and gone, Cooper's ever-prepared cousin had an umbrella in his hand.

Cooper had arranged for Reece to come on board and look over the books this evening, which was supposed to be Allie's night off. He had promised to handle all the post-cruise business, and he would—as soon as his stomach unknotted.

He still couldn't believe he'd hit a rock.

He'd been so sure he knew what he was doing, so intent on proving to Allie that he could do her job as well as she could. He'd figured that by the time the legal battle for the *Dragonfly* was over, he would have learned anything he needed to about running a charter service, and Allie Bateman would be evicted and on her way.

But clearly that wasn't the case.

He wondered if he could hire Allie as his pilot. She would soon need a job. But he rejected that possibility, just as he'd done the first time it occurred to him. Once he wrested the boat away from her she wasn't likely to want to work for him. In fact, she would probably go to work for one of the other charter businesses and do her damnedest to run him out of business.

"How'd it go?" Reece asked as Cooper secured the boat.

"Not so good," he admitted.

He helped their passengers disembark and carried their cooler of fish as far as the dock. The men were in high spirits, even the one who'd been seasick. They promised Cooper and Allie they'd be back next year.

"It sounds like the customers had a good time," Reece observed as he followed Cooper onto the boat. She was bobbing up and down so fiercely, they had to time their move just right to avoid falling in the water. "How did the beer thing work out?"

"The passengers seemed to like it."

"Hello, Allie," Reece said politely.

Allie was busy emptying the trash barrel, and she barely looked up. "Hello…Reece, is it?"

"Yes, ma'am. Let me help you with that. This was my job when I used to visit Uncle Johnny."

"The only thing Johnny would trust him to do," Cooper added.

"Oh…thank you."

"Allie, this is your night off, remember?" Cooper said. "We'll handle all the cleanup and restock provisions." He would also have to take the boat to be refueled and to clean out the holding tank. He felt a little jittery at the idea, though it was just around the corner. "What's on the schedule for tomorrow?"

"Nothing, unfortunately," Allie replied, "but we should still stock up in case there's a last-minute booking."

"Do you often have idle days?" Reece asked.

Allie immediately went on the defensive. "It's still the off-season, and I'm only now getting the business back up to full speed. Johnny couldn't work the last few weeks of his illness."

Cooper felt a pang of loss and guilt. Though Allie would

never believe him, he'd have been here to take care of Uncle Johnny if he'd known the man was dying.

He'd always thought there would be time.

"We're still well-stocked with soft drinks," Allie said, pulling them back to business. "But we need cold cuts and fruit. Bread we can buy tomorrow morning at Romanelli's Bakery, when it's freshest."

"Don't worry," Cooper told her. "We'll handle everything. You just go out and have a good time. But before you leave, can you show Reece your financial records? He's here to go over the books." He tensed, expecting her to balk.

"Of course," she said smoothly. "But I'm not going anywhere. I'll fix myself some dinner and read in my bunk."

That seemed a strange choice to Cooper. She'd been on the boat all day. Didn't she want to get out? Maybe she wanted to keep an eye on things, in case he and Reece had in mind to walk off with the silverware or something.

Allie led them downstairs and to the rear of the boat. She unlocked the hatch that led to the captain's quarters.

Johnny's presence was still strong here, and a wave of nostalgia washed over Cooper. The cabin looked exactly the same as he remembered, right down to the picture of St. Brendan the Navigator, patron saint of sailors, bolted to the wall. Even his pipe smoke lingered.

The finality of Uncle Johnny's passing hit him hard in the gut. The old man wouldn't emerge from some hatch, whistling a jaunty tune, pipe clenched in his teeth and a glass of Scotch in his hand. He'd always been a drinking man, but before Aunt Pat's death, spirits were strictly for after the boat was in port.

And Aunt Pat. Cooper had been focusing so much on

Johnny he hadn't given much thought to her, because she'd died so many years ago, but memories of her lurked at the edges of his mind. She'd been a hard-living, wiry woman with a sense of adventure every bit as strong as her husband's. She'd had a tattoo of a sailboat on her shoulder long before tattoos were stylish.

She'd been a heckuva cook and she taught her nephews to play poker like pros.

"Something wrong?" Allie asked.

He realized he'd just been standing in the doorway, frozen. He shook himself. "Just remembering."

Allie went to a small desk in the corner of the cabin, opened a drawer, and pulled out an old-fashioned ledger book as well as four checkbooks and a cash box.

She laid out the checkbooks on the desktop. "Business account, Johnny's personal account—which has been closed, and my two personal accounts—savings and checking. You're welcome to work in here, but you'd have more room in the salon," she said.

"Won't we be in your way in here?" Reece asked.

"I don't use this room except to do bookkeeping. I sleep in the V-berth. Will you need anything else?"

Reece had opened the cover of the ledger book and was looking at it with a strange expression on his face. "You don't have your records on computer?"

Allie shrugged. "Never felt the need. Remington Charters' accounting is pretty simple, and as you can see I don't have room for a computer. The salt air eats them up pretty bad, anyway."

How did anyone survive in this day and age without a computer? Cooper wondered.

"We might want to wait until tomorrow to get fueled

up," Allie said on her way out of the cabin. "The storms will pass by then."

"Okay." Cooper couldn't deny he was relieved.

He knew he should get to the grocery store before it closed. He'd quickly discovered that during the off-season Port Clara rolled up the sidewalks at night. Only the bars and the Quicky Mart stayed open past seven o'clock.

But he was curious to know what was in the ledger. If they could find evidence that Allie mismanaged funds, it would help their case.

After spending a couple of days with Allie, he couldn't picture her siphoning off funds and socking them away in a Swiss bank account. And what would she spend it on here? She clearly didn't have a lot of expensive clothes or jewelry, and he'd seen her car, an ancient Isuzu Rodeo.

They took Allie's suggestion and moved to the salon where they could spread out a bit. Cooper helped himself to a beer and settled into a comfortable chair while Reece began studying the ledger in earnest, making notations on a legal pad every so often.

But watching Reece frown and scribble and punch numbers into his calculator got pretty boring after a minute or so, and Cooper found his gaze straying toward the galley, where Allie was fixing herself some dinner. One of the passengers—a guy who'd flirted with Allie at every opportunity—had gifted her with a small snapper fillet on his departure, and it appeared she was marinating it in some concoction.

She fixed herself a salad—spinach, tomatoes, cucumbers—then tossed the fish on an indoor grill, adding spices from a well-stocked rack.

"Allie apparently knows how to cook," Cooper observed quietly.

"Mm-hmm."

"I want to offer our passengers a gourmet meal. Maybe Allie could be our cook."

Reece looked up. "Are you insane? If we win this lawsuit, she won't want to work for us, she'll want to kill us."

Cooper sighed. "Yeah, I guess you're right." He'd just needed someone to confirm the conclusion he'd already drawn.

He resumed his study of Allie, fully appreciating the length and shapeliness of her tanned legs. She'd abandoned her deck shoes, and Cooper saw that her toenails were painted bright red. That little feminine detail intrigued him. She didn't wear makeup—not that she needed any—and her idea of a hairstyle was to pull her long red hair into a clip on top of her head. She obviously saw no need for designer clothes, preferring those ancient cut-off jeans and tank shirts. Her nails were short and utilitarian and her hands work-roughened.

But the toenails said she hadn't forgotten she was a woman.

Cooper wished *he* could forget she was a woman. Every time he looked at her he got distracted, and that was a bad thing.

Heather had distracted him, though in a different way. She was nearly six feet tall with a model's body and a slick, magazine cover look about her. When she entered a room, all heads turned, and she had used that power, along with her wide-eyed innocent act, to divert attention from her nefarious activities.

She had started out stealing knickknacks and baubles from his house, and then the considerably more valuable stuff from his parents' home. His parents had actually fired a hapless housekeeper over the missing items.

Emboldened by her success with minor thefts, she had progressed to stealing credit card numbers and shopping on the Internet.

Cooper admitted it—he never looked over his bill that carefully. He used it for everything, so the list of charges went on for pages. So long as the total didn't seem out of line, he just paid it.

He'd finally caught on when an eight-hundred-dollar charge from a designer shoe store caught his eye. He started looking closer at his bill and was horrified to find a half-dozen charges for purchases he knew nothing about.

He knew immediately who'd done it. At first he was inclined to believe he'd somehow given her implicit permission to use his Visa. They were, after all, engaged.

He spoke to her about it, and if she'd just simply admitted she'd done it, apologized, and promised not to do it again, she would have gotten away with it.

But she denied any knowledge of the mystery purchases and tried to blame it on his parents' cleaning lady, who had become a convenient scapegoat.

After launching a full investigation, the depth of her thievery came to light. She'd siphoned off thousands and thousands of dollars—not just from his credit card, but his bank accounts and those of his parents. She wasn't just a greedy woman with a shopping addiction, she was a skilled con artist.

Turned out her name wasn't even Heather.

She'd disappeared before Cooper could gather together enough facts to have her arrested, probably living high in the Cayman Islands on his money.

When he turned his attention back to Reece, Cooper saw that his cousin was no longer studying the ledger. He had his eyes closed and his hands extended beside him, as if to hold himself upright.

"Reece?"

"This wasn't a good idea," he said without opening his eyes. "It's like reading in a car. These records will require several hours of study, and I can't do it on this moving boat."

"You can't take all my financial stuff off the boat," Allie called from the galley where she sat at a fold-down table, eating her dinner. Apparently she'd been listening. "I might never see it again."

"We'll take it and have it photocopied," Cooper said. "We'll bring it right back."

She looked at her watch, an ancient windup Timex. "Copy shop's closed."

"We'll do it first thing in the morning."

Reece stood and staggered toward the hatch. "You guys work it out. I need fresh air."

Allie stood and came into the salon. "You can't take all my financial stuff away," she said again. "That's ludicrous."

"Allie. I wouldn't destroy your property. I don't need to cheat."

"Cheating's the only way you'll win."

They stood staring at each other, both of them breathing hard, and Cooper felt an insane urge to pull her into his arms and kiss her into agreeing with him.

He couldn't take her records without her permission, so he backed down a fraction. "We'll make a list of everything I remove from the premises, and we'll both sign it. When I return everything, we'll tear up the list."

She thought about his offer for a few moments, and finally she relaxed a bit. "I guess that's fair."

Allie could think of no graceful way to refuse Cooper's request without sounding like she had something to hide. But as she signed her name to the list of items he was removing, she felt like she was signing a bargain with the devil.

Would she ever see her carefully maintained financial history again? Yes, she'd made copies, but that didn't completely lay her mind at ease. Cooper could trip on his way up the dock and send all that paperwork flying into the water. He could have a wreck on the way home and the papers could burn up.

He could orchestrate any number of ways to destroy the records once he realized they proved she'd sunk her life savings into this boat. She'd been Johnny's partner, which gave him clear and reasonable motivation for leaving her the boat in his will.

That was something Cooper Remington did not want a judge to see.

WHEN ALLIE WOKE UP THE NEXT morning, she knew immediately something was wrong.

The storm that had blown in had kept her awake much of the night. The boat had pitched and the wind had howled and whistled through the cracks in the windows. Some of the seals were broken, and she'd had to place rolled-up towels around a few windows to keep the rain from coming in.

But all was quiet now. The dawn sky looked clear.

Still, something was definitely wrong, and it wasn't until Allie came more fully awake that she realized what it was.

The boat sat too low in the water, even accounting for low tide, and it listed to one side.

Allie flew out of her berth in her pajamas and went directly to the hatch in the galley that led down to the engines. When she opened it, she nearly fainted.

The *Dragonfly* was taking on water.

When they'd hit that rock, they must have done more damage than she'd thought. She'd checked last night and hadn't seen any water coming in, but it had been too dark and the water too choppy for her to get in the water and inspect the hull. She ran to put on her waders, then vaulted down into the engine compartment and switched on the pump. But that was just a stopgap measure; she had to get the boat into dry dock immediately.

She quickly changed clothes, then dialed Cooper's cell phone as she clamored up to the deck to cast off. It wasn't that she felt any obligation to notify him; nor did she have any desire to rub his nose in the fact he'd wrecked her boat. But she was keenly aware of the agreement she had made not to sail without a Remington on board until their case had been decided. Cooper would use any excuse he could come up with to give her trouble or argue that she was defying a court order.

Unfortunately, she got his voice mail. "Cooper, it's Allie. The *Dragonfly* has sprung a leak and I'm taking her to Sinclair Marine, about three miles east. I have to do it now or she'll sink."

Allie didn't have any of the other Remingtons' numbers. She tried the B and B—she would have Miss Greer drag Cooper out of bed if necessary. But Miss Greer turned the ringer down on her phone at night because people called at strange hours. So Allie got no answer there, either. She left another message, then made one more phone call to Otis Sinclair, letting him know she was coming and to get ready for her.

At least the engines started.

She eased the *Dragonfly* out of her slip and turned east for her slow trip up the coast, limping along and praying the boat didn't sink.

## Chapter Six

Cooper hadn't slept well. Memories of hitting that rock mingled with restless dreams about Allie and her gorgeous legs, and the mistrust he'd seen in those green eyes.

He was up before light and was glad to find Reece awake, too. They gathered up Remington Charters' financial records, chucked them into Cooper's briefcase, and left the B and B before their restlessness awakened any of the other guests or Miss Greer, who was a little bit scary first thing in the morning before she'd had her coffee.

Of course, the copy shop wasn't open yet.

"Let's go get some breakfast at the Old Salt," Cooper suggested. "By the time we're done, the copy shop will be open and we can return Allie's records to her."

"Miss Greer will be offended if we don't eat her breakfast," Reece pointed out as they climbed into Cooper's rented BMW. Cooper had hired a neighbor kid to drive his car from New York to Texas, but it wouldn't arrive for a few days.

"I don't know about you, but Miss Greer has a strange idea of what constitutes a good breakfast."

"Oh, I always go out and get something else after I eat her itty-bitty pastries," Reece said. "I just wouldn't want to hurt her feelings. She's awfully proud of those cream puffs, or whatever they are."

*Whatever* was right. Cooper found them nearly inedible. "Miss Greer will survive. We can't be the first guests to turn down breakfast." Leave it to Reece to worry about offending someone they hardly knew. He'd once dated a woman for six months when he saw no future in it because he hadn't wanted to hurt her feelings by breaking up with her. "She's not anybody's grandmother, she's someone we do business with."

"She's probably *someone's* grandmother," Reece pointed out.

"She's never been married, and you're too nice."

"You've got a heart like a rock."

"At least no one can stomp on it."

It was a familiar argument, and Reece just rolled his eyes.

Even at this early hour the Old Salt was packed because they served the best breakfast in town. But Cooper and Reece managed to find a table on the deck. They ordered another decadent breakfast for Cooper and oatmeal for Reece.

Cooper took a long, satisfying sip of his coffee, leaned back in his chair, and cast his eyes toward the marina, wondering if he would catch any glimpses of Allie this morning. Did she sleep late when she didn't have an outing scheduled, or was she an early riser like him?

"You sure know how to pick 'em," Reece said.

"What?"

"Women. Your last girlfriend was a con artist, and now you've got the hots for a woman who hates your guts."

"She doesn't hate me. I mean, I don't have the hots for her, as you so charmingly put it. *And* she doesn't hate me."

"You're trying to take away her livelihood. You think

she'll put you on her Christmas card list? And if you don't have a thing for her, why are you always staring at her? You're looking for her right this second."

"No, actually, what I'm looking for is our boat. And I don't see it."

That got Reece's attention. He swiveled his chair around and peered off toward the marina.

"Am I crazy," Cooper said, "or is the *Dragonfly*'s slip empty?"

"My God. You're right."

They stared at each other.

"She stole our boat."

"Don't jump to conclusions," said Reece, always the voice of reason. "Maybe she just went to get gas and maintenance."

Cooper was already reaching for his phone, intending to call 9-1-1 or the Coast Guard, or whoever it was you called to report a stolen boat. But he stopped before actually dialing. Allie had said something about getting fuel this morning. "Let's go check at the marina."

But Reece was staring out to sea. "Isn't that the *Dragonfly?* Heading away from the marina?"

Damn it. It was. Cooper dialed. "I want to report a stolen boat."

He explained the situation to the patient emergency operator. Reece put some money on the table for the breakfast they would never eat, and they took off. It looked as if Allie was staying close to the coast. They could follow along the coast road in their car and maintain visual contact until the Coast Guard could catch up with her.

"I knew she was up to no good," Cooper said as they ran to his BMW. "She probably realized the jig was up once we took a good look at those financials. I'll bet there's evidence she was skimming the profits, embezzling. She's probably been socking it all away in a Swiss bank account, and now she's going to sell the boat to some black-market boat dealer who'll use it to run drugs, and Allie will be on the first plane to Brazil."

"That's a very interesting scenario you've worked out," Reece commented as Cooper drove like a maniac to the main road that paralleled the coast.

"Can you see her?"

"Yes. Slow down. You know, she's not moving very fast for a woman with a hot boat. And why wouldn't she set a course farther out from shore?"

"Not all criminals are smart."

They followed along, sometimes pulling to the side of the road to let the *Dragonfly* catch up with them, sometimes zooming ahead when waterfront structures blocked their view.

"Allie doesn't strike me as stupid," Reece said.

"Yeah, well…you know, I was almost starting to like her. I was starting to feel bad about evicting her from the boat. I was actually starting to wonder if maybe Johnny had misled her, made her promises so she wouldn't leave him. Just goes to show how gullible I am. She almost had me with her devoted-employee act."

"I think I see a Coast Guard cutter."

"Really? That was fast." Cooper had mixed feelings about seeing Allie dragged off in handcuffs. She was a heckuva sailor. He'd been looking forward to sailing with her until their court date. Well, he'd have to learn as he went.

"They're still pretty far away," Reece said, "but they're heading straight for the *Dragonfly*."

Cooper had to keep his eyes on the congested roadway,

so he relied on Reece to report everything. "What's the *Dragonfly* doing?"

"Just putting along at about three knots. Looks like maybe she's heading into that little cove up ahead. There's a big sign—Sinclair Marine."

"Maybe it's a chop shop for boats. They'll take off the name and the serial numbers and replace 'em with—oh, no."

"What?"

"The sign, underneath Sinclair Marine. What does it say?"

Reece squinted. "Fiberglass Boat Repair, Dry Dock."

A terrible suspicion occurred to Cooper. "Did I tell you about hitting the rock yesterday?"

ALLIE WAVED TO THE COAST GUARD cutter to let them know she was okay. They probably could see the boat listed to one side and had come to check on her.

"*Dragonfly*. This is the U.S. Coast Guard."

Good Lord. They were calling to her on a bullhorn. What was wrong with the radio?

She waved again and smiled, since she could see one officer had binoculars trained on her.

"Cut your engines and prepare to be boarded."

What? She complied immediately. She never messed with the Coast Guard.

The cutter pulled alongside her and two stern-looking officers leaped aboard with their weapons drawn.

"All parties on deck *now*. Keep your hands where we can see them."

"It's just me," Allie called from the bridge. "I'm coming down the ladder. I don't have any weapons, promise."

The two officers met her as she descended. "We have a report this boat has been stolen."

*Cooper.* "Hmm. Well, since I am the owner of the boat—you'll find it registered to me—I hardly think that's true. I am, however, in violation of a court order. The ownership is in dispute and I'm not supposed to sail it on my own. But it's an emergency. As you can probably tell, the boat is taking on water and I'm headed into Sinclair Marine for repairs. I left a message for Cooper Remington on his cell phone.

"Cooper Remington," she repeated. "That is who made the stolen-boat report, right?"

The officers both took a step back, giving her some space. "Have a seat," one of them said. "I'll be right back."

He stepped off to confer with his captain.

"See that man on the dock?" Allie said to the other officer, pointing toward shore. "That's Mr. Sinclair. He's expecting me." She waved to him, and he waved back.

The other officer returned. "Apparently there's been a misunderstanding. We'll escort you in."

Yeah, now that she was a hundred feet from her destination.

She wasn't too surprised to see Cooper and Reece standing on the dock waiting for her as she pulled the *Dragonfly* into a slip where a hoist would haul her out of the water.

"I'll need to gather a few things," she called to Otis, who had guided her in. "Just keep her from sinking until I can pack up. How long till you can get to her?"

Otis Sinclair was a portly old man whose family had owned this business for three generations. He did the best work and charged the fairest price of anyone in these parts. Consequently he was always booked.

He gave her a worried look as he chomped on his unlit cigar. "Be a week, at least."

She groaned. A week with no work, and that was assuming the repairs would be routine. But she had an even worse problem. With the *Dragonfly* in dry dock, she had no home.

She quickly gathered up a few clothes and toiletries and stuffed them into a backpack. She also unloaded what little perishable food was left in the fridge and put it in a couple of plastic grocery sacks. At least she wouldn't starve for a day or two.

By the time she disembarked, one of the Coast Guard officers was in serious discussion with the Remington boys. Good. She hoped he gave them hell for jumping to conclusions and wasting the Coast Guard's time.

When he saw her, the officer broke away from his conversation and offered her a dazzling smile. "Ms. Bateman. Sorry to have inconvenienced you. My name's Jimmy, and if you need anything you don't hesitate to call." He handed her a card.

Behind him, Cooper rolled his eyes.

The officer rejoined his boat and took off, and Allie sauntered up to her nemesis. "Check your voicemail lately?"

At least he had the good grace to look embarrassed. "Um, yeah. Sorry about that."

"Is that all you have to say? 'Sorry about that'? First you knock a hole in my boat, and then you try to have me arrested, and that's the best you can do?"

"I'll pay for the repairs."

"I'm counting on that." Otherwise she would have to make an insurance claim, and that took time.

"It was an honest mistake."

"You actually thought I was stealing my own boat!"

"He thought you were going to sell it to a drug dealer," Reece added, looking like he was about to burst out laughing.

Cooper shot him a scathing look. "You're not helping. Look, Allie, let me make it up to you. Can I buy you breakfast?"

Like that would solve anything when she was homeless? "You can give me a ride to the Bella Motel," she said. It was kind of a dive, but it was the cheapest digs in Port Clara and they rented by the week. "I need to establish a base of operations and start calling the customers who are booked for the next seven days—at least—and try to reschedule or find them an alternative charter service."

"I'll help you make calls," he offered as he took her backpack from her as well as the bag of food. "Why don't you stay at the Sunsetter?"

"Because I can't afford the Sunsetter," she said pointedly.

"It's on me. This is all my fault. I'll take care of all your expenses until the *Dragonfly* is back on her keel."

"It's kind of you, but I don't want to be your kept woman. The Bella Motel is fine."

Reece snorted. Obviously he was finding the situation amusing.

She did, too, in a way. It was almost worth suffering through this disaster, just to see the great Cooper Remington eating crow. Almost, but not quite.

COOPER SLOWED DOWN AS HE approached the Bella Motel, which was anything but *bella*. Probably built in the 1950s, it looked as if it hadn't been updated since. The U-shaped, one-story building squatted in a semi-industrial area, and the sign indicated you could rent by the hour.

"Allie, you can't stay here. This doesn't even look safe."

"I have a gun, remember?"

"Stay at the Sunsetter. I'll pay for it."

"It's not necessary. Anyway, I wouldn't feel comfortable living under the same roof as you."

"Come on, admit it, you don't really hate me. In fact, you're starting to like me a little bit."

"When hell freezes over."

Reece cleared his throat. "Maybe I should leave you two lovebirds alone."

Despite her protests, Cooper drove away from the Bella Motel and took her to the Sunsetter. "This is where you're staying if it's on my dime."

"Fine," she snapped. "But we damn well better be too late for breakfast, because I'm not eating those cream puffs."

"WON'T MISS GREER SKIN YOU alive for raiding her refrigerator?" Allie asked later that afternoon as Sara put together a plate of cheese and crackers.

Allie was starving. She had spent the past couple of hours shuffling her various bookings, rescheduling a few but mostly placing them with other charter services. She hated to lose the business. A couple of them were longtime customers.

She'd been so busy she'd forgotten lunch, but Sara, always watching out for her friends, insisted Allie eat something.

"Don't worry, this is from my private stash," Sara said. "Miss Greer gives me one shelf in the pantry and one in the fridge."

"It's probably more room than I have on the *Dragonfly* for my personal groceries. I could get used to having this big kitchen to cook in." And the enormous shower with its twin sprays, and the huge four-poster bed with three feather pillows. She could hardly wait to sleep in it tonight. Though it galled her that Cooper had manipulated her into staying where he thought she should stay, she wasn't really sorry he'd won that argument.

She told herself all the time that she was a simple person with simple needs. She needed food, a dry bunk, and she needed to be near the ocean where she could see the sky and smell the salt air.

But suddenly being thrust into the Sunsetter's luxurious surroundings reminded her she had other needs. Like a need for scented lotion, and lipstick, and a place to go where lipstick wouldn't look out of place. Silk panties… and someone to appreciate them.

"So how was your trip, other than the porn film?" Allie asked after three crackers put a dent in her hunger. "We haven't talked much since you got back."

Sara wrinkled her nose. "Not worth talking about. Guy turned out to be a jerk."

"Oh, so there was a guy involved."

"Isn't there always?" Sara crunched down on a cracker.

"Do you ever think about settling down with just one?"

Sara shrugged. "Nah. I'm too restless for that. Besides, I've never found a guy who didn't get on my nerves after a while." She paused and looked out the window, deliberately not meeting Allie's gaze. "But I do want children."

"Really?"

Sara stood suddenly. "I forgot to offer you something to drink. Juice?"

"Sure, whatever."

"Don't you want kids someday?" Sara asked.

"No room on the boat for kids."

"But you don't have to live on the boat forever. Most of the other captains have homes in town. They have wives and kids."

"Maybe someday," Allie said lightly, though she wasn't really comfortable talking about this and wished she hadn't brought it up. Now wasn't a good time to think about living a more mainstream life. If her commitment to Remington Charters wavered even a little, she was afraid Cooper would find the chink in her armor and exploit it.

"So tell me more about the Remingtons. I made them breakfast this morning, and they didn't *seem* like devils."

"Appearances are deceiving. They ignored Johnny for twenty years, remember. But as soon as he died they gathered around like vultures."

"Have you asked them why they stayed away?"

"There's no good reason not to see your family while they're alive."

"What about your uncle? You haven't seen him in, like, ten years."

"That's different! Uncle Daniel is a thief, a criminal. He took my inheritance away from me and squandered it. I don't ever want to see him again, and I damn sure won't come calling when he dies."

"But what if he left you something in his will?" Sara persisted. "You wouldn't take it? You wouldn't figure he owes it to you?"

Hmm. She'd never thought of it that way.

"I'm just saying that you don't really know what their family history is."

"All I know is that Johnny had no intention of giving them the *Dragonfly*. I know it and they know it. They're pulling legal tricks to try to defraud me out of my boat."

"I'm on your side in this." Sara squeezed Allie's shoulders. "Don't worry about that. But it's possible the Remingtons aren't evil incarnate. Not everything is black and white."

Allie didn't want to hear this. It was easier to avoid shades of gray.

With her hunger temporarily sated, Allie grabbed her backpack and headed out, hoping to escape the Sunsetter without running into any Remingtons, but wouldn't you know it, she stumbled upon a whole nest of them in the parlor.

Reece had her ledgers and other papers spread out over a card table; he was so engrossed in his audit that he didn't see her try to sneak through to the front door. But Cooper and the other cousin—Max?—saw her. They both looked up from their study of a laptop computer; legal pads and what looked like reference books were scattered across a coffee table.

"Allie, where are you going?" Cooper asked.

"To find work. While the *Dragonfly*'s in dry dock, I still have bills to pay." She was hoping one of the other captains would hire her on as a temporary deckhand or cook.

Heck, she'd even hire on a commercial fishing vessel, though most of those guys were superstitious about allowing a woman on their ships.

She intended to intercept the pleasure boats as they came in for the evening, and the commercial boats as they prepared to sail for night fishing.

"Have you had anything to eat today?" Cooper asked. "I did promise you a meal."

"I just ate. Another time." She noticed, then, that Max had a fat lip and a black eye. "What happened to you?"

He flashed her an easy grin. "Your neighbor took a swing at me. He thought I was getting too familiar with his wife."

Ugh. Scott Simone. Allie didn't know how Jane put up with the guy—he was a complete jerk. Then again, it gave

Allie a petty grain of satisfaction that one of the Remingtons had been on the receiving end of Scott's legendary temper.

Maybe that explained why Jane and Scott had departed so abruptly. Scott had probably insisted they return to Houston. He knew Jane loved her time in Port Clara, so he punished her by dragging her away from it. It wasn't the first time Scott had accused Jane of flirting inappropriately with another man, though Allie knew her neighbor was just friendly, nothing more.

"Why don't you work for me this week," Cooper said. "It's my fault you don't have any money coming in."

"You've got to be kidding." When she realized he wasn't, she asked, "What in the world could I do for you?"

"Consultant. We have a lot to learn about the charter fishing business. Max is putting together a preliminary marketing plan, but we could use your input."

"Putting together a marketing plan for a business you might or might not own."

Cooper shrugged one of his broad shoulders. "It's a risk I'm willing to take."

Clearly he was confident he would prevail. What did he know that she didn't? Her will was dated after his. End of story. Wasn't it?

Curious about their marketing plans, she sidled over to the coffee table. They'd apparently been studying a number of brochures and magazine ads for rival charter services.

She picked up a tri-fold piece of paper with some crude sketches, which she guessed was a mock-up for their own brochure.

"That's really rough," Max apologized. "I'm a concept man, not an artist."

"The last word on luxury charter fishing," Allie read, her

voice dripping with sarcasm. "Champagne and starlight cruise? Gourmet meal included?"

"We think Remington Charters can pull in a much larger profit if we tap the luxury travel market."

"In Port Clara."

"Why not? We've got three major metropolitan areas within easy driving distance. If we can give them more luxury for less money than they can get in Corpus Christi or Galveston, why wouldn't they come to us? But we have to let them know we're here. How much money do you invest in advertising and marketing?"

Not much, especially lately when she was merely trying to keep her head above water.

"It's all spelled out in the records," she said evasively, nodding toward Reece.

"Not enough, I'm guessing," Cooper said. "Your competitors have splashy ads in every travel and tourist publication out there. You have only a few. And the Web site is woefully out of date."

"The logo's really good, though," Max observed. "Who designed it?"

"It was my idea, but Jane designed it. You know Jane. Her husband slugged you."

Max seemed to deflate. "Oh. Guess I can't hire her, then."

"Max is starting his own advertising and P.R. firm," Cooper explained. "Remington Charters will be its number-one client."

"One of many," Max hastened to add.

"So what do you say?" Cooper looked at her expectantly. "Want to lend us your expertise? I'll make it worth your while."

"Why would I want to help you?"

"Because," Cooper said, and she could tell he relished making his final point, "if you win, you get to keep whatever we come up with. Free. It won't be any use to us."

That brought her up short. She'd always wanted to do a full-blown marketing campaign, but she hadn't known where to begin. Aside from the capital investment it would require, Johnny had been against it, anyway—he said they kept their schedule pretty full without running a lot of fancy ads.

But if these Ivy League-educated Remington boys could come up with ways to increase profits without alienating their longtime customers…she'd be a fool not to benefit from their expertise in areas where she had none.

"How much are you willing to pay me?" she asked.

"Whatever you'd make as a deckhand, plus twenty-five percent."

"You don't know what I make as a deckhand," she pointed out.

"See, that's one of the reasons we need you. We may need to hire on some help, and we have no idea what sort of pay to offer them."

It was tempting to take them for a ride, but in the end she named a figure she probably could have earned working freelance.

Cooper nodded. "Plus twenty-five percent. You there, with the calculator—what does that work out to?"

Reece looked up a bit foggily. "Huh?"

"Never mind him," Max said. "He's deep into his facts and figures. We'll sort it out."

Working side by side with Cooper for a week might be foolhardy. What if he had some ulterior motive, some way to use her agreeability to gather evidence against her? But she looked at it from every angle, and she couldn't find a reason to turn down the offer.

"Do we have a deal?" Cooper stood and offered her his hand.

Allie hesitated only slightly before clasping his hand in hers. "Deal." A tingle of awareness buzzed through her at his touch, and she almost hated to release his hand. Why did he have to be so good-looking? Why did he have to have that charming smile and those twinkly blue eyes? She would have a much easier job despising him if he was as cold and arrogant as he'd first appeared.

"Our first order of business is to buy you some new clothes. Not that the Daisy Dukes aren't attractive, but we don't want to start a riot at the trade show."

"Trade show?"

"This weekend, in Houston. Vacation Expo. You and I are going to work it. Together."

## Chapter Seven

Cooper enjoyed the look of consternation on his new employee's beautiful face.

Reece and Max both thought he was slightly insane for wanting to hire Allie. But everything he'd told her was true. If the court awarded her the boat and the charter business, she would benefit from all the work they were doing. And if Cooper and his cousins prevailed, well, they had one week of Allie's cooperation, which they sorely needed.

They had an incredible amount of work to get done before the weekend. It was a stroke of luck they'd heard about the trade show from Miss Greer, who paid to participate in a booth run by a bed-and-breakfast association. But it sounded like exactly the sort of place Remington Charters could get good exposure to people who were actually planning vacations, and he hadn't wanted to toss away the opportunity, even if it meant they had to scramble to get ready in time.

"You want me to buy new clothes?" Allie repeated, looking at him as if he was insane.

"I'll pay for them. Company expense. I was thinking something nautical."

"You're going to dress me in a sailor outfit and turn me into a trade-show booth bunny."

"Hey, don't be insulted. All the booths at trade shows hire beautiful models—you'll see when we get there. We're fortunate to have our talent in-house."

Allie looked down at herself. "I'm fine the way I am."

"Did someone say shopping?" Sara entered the living room wearing sunglasses and a straw hat, a huge denim purse slung over her shoulder. "Allie, if you're going to shop, take me along. You can't trust a man's shopping advice."

Cooper sensed an ally in Sara. Though she wasn't exactly a fashion plate, she did have a certain style about her with her big, dangly earrings and bright, multicolored skirt. She certainly had Reece's attention. The moment she'd appeared, Reece had lifted his gaze from his books and he hadn't taken his eyes off her since.

Interesting.

Reece had been adamant that he wasn't relocating to Port Clara, but maybe there was a way to keep him here after all.

The three youngest Remington cousins had always stuck together. And though he and Max would carry on without Reece if they had to, it wouldn't be the same.

"All right," Allie said, "I'll go shopping if you insist. I guess it wouldn't hurt me to buy a few new clothes, especially on the Remington dime. But you back me up," she said to Sara. "Don't you let him push me into buying some ridiculous, low-cut, nautical streetwalker outfit."

That was sort of what Cooper had in mind, something form-fitting and low-cut to show off Allie's figure. He'd have to see what he could talk her into.

Port Clara had one mall, if you could call it that, a collection of about twenty stores, mostly tourist-related. But the mall was anchored by a small department store and a couple of high-end boutiques.

Sara immediately zeroed in on the most expensive-looking of the stores. "This one," she said. "I love the clothes in here." She grabbed Allie by the arm and dragged her in, ignoring Cooper completely. Well, perhaps shopping just wasn't something men really understood. He didn't select his own clothes, after all. He had a personal shopper who knew his tastes and took care of all that for him.

But he did know what looked good on a woman. Sara veered to a rack of summery dresses first.

"No dresses!" Allie declared. "I don't do dresses. Besides, I'm supposed to be the captain of a fishing boat. It wouldn't be seemly. If I have to dress up, a pair of trousers and some kind of shirt will be fine."

Sara looked disappointed, but she peered around the store until she saw what she wanted, then made a beeline for it. "This would look fabulous on you," she said, grabbing a pair of white pants with a short jacket that matched. "And let's see, how about a striped tee to wear underneath? That would be nautical."

It also wouldn't be sexy. Cooper looked around the store himself, trying to find something that matched his idea of what Allie should wear at the trade show. A couple of minutes later he found it: a blue-and-white halter dress with a plunging neckline. It had little anchors embroidered on the straps and around the bottom.

If he could get her to try it on, maybe to humor him, she would see how good it looked.

"What size do you wear?" Sara was asking.

"I don't know," Allie answered.

"What do you mean, you don't know?"

Allie shrugged. "I never go shopping. I don't think I've bought any new clothes this century other than the uniform shirts I put the logo on, and I got those mail order. I think they're a medium."

Sara looked Allie up and down. "About a six, I'd say. We'll just have to try."

A sales clerk showed them to a dressing room. Cooper handed the halter dress to the clerk when she came back out. "Could you take this in to the redhead? I think she might like it."

The clerk looked skeptical. "Didn't she say no dresses?"

"She might change her mind," Cooper said hopefully.

The clerk took the dress and disappeared again into the fitting rooms. He didn't hear any screams of outrage, so he kept his fingers crossed. Having Allie in their booth at the trade show was a stroke of genius. Even if she wore a potato sack, with that gorgeous red hair and green eyes, she would pull people in—at least the men.

He wasn't sure about advertising she was the captain. He still felt that people would be more comfortable with a man in charge. Sexist of him, he knew, but that was the way of the world. But he could work on that part of their plan later. One step at a time.

A few minutes later, Sara dragged Allie out of the dressing room. He had insisted he must see her in the clothes before making any decisions.

He hadn't expected to like the white outfit, but now that he saw it on her, he realized Sara knew her stuff. The T-shirt's scoop neck gave him an intriguing glimpse of the shadow between Allie's full breasts, and the way those pants hugged her hips made his mouth go dry.

"Doesn't she look fabulous, Cooper?" Sara said.

Allie was looking anywhere and everywhere but at him. She was actually trying to pull away from Sara, trying to escape back into the dressing room like a gopher seeking the safety of its burrow.

"She does, in fact, look fabulous." His voice was low, laced with innuendo, though he hadn't meant for it to come out like that.

Allie blushed in the way only a redhead can. "All right, fine, let's buy it already." She slipped Sara's clutches and darted to safety.

"What about the dress?" Cooper asked.

"Haven't gotten her into it yet," Sara whispered, "but I'm working on it."

ALLIE GAZED AT HER REFLECTION in the mirror and wasn't quite sure what to think. She hadn't seen herself in anything but denim and T-shirts since she'd graduated from baby clothes. She was a tomboy through and through. Her mother had practically had to tie her down to get her into proper school clothes.

Even for Johnny's funeral, she'd borrowed a pair of black jeans and a sober shirt from Sara, and she certainly hadn't bothered to look at herself in a mirror. Matter of fact, she hadn't seen herself in a full-length mirror in…she didn't know how long.

"You look great!" Sara tucked in the tag at the back of the halter dress. "Cooper's right, you could be a model."

"Oh, Sara, get real."

"No, really, you're a knockout. Little makeup, some earrings…I'd give anything to have your boobs. Well, you know what I mean."

"It shows too much chest," Allie argued, though she had to admit she kind of liked how she looked. She'd never thought of herself as sexy, or even very pretty. Growing up she'd always been "that redheaded Bateman girl," with no figure to speak of and too many freckles.

But she actually did have a figure now.

"I really would be a booth bunny if I wore this to the trade show." The dress fit as if it had been tailor-made for her. The soft knit clung to her every curve and moved when she did; the daring neckline showed more of her chest than even her bathing suit did.

"Cooper picked this out?"

"That's what the salesgirl said. Oh, Allie, you have to buy it. If not for the trade show, then wear it to a party or something."

"Cooper isn't going to buy me clothes to wear to any party—as if I ever go to parties."

"But you look so pretty."

"No. Let's find another top to wear with the white pants."

It wasn't difficult to find a blouse that coordinated with the white pants, and soon Cooper was at the register paying for their purchases while Sara looked over the purses.

"What about shoes?" she asked.

"I can wear my white deck shoes."

"No! You'll ruin the whole outfit. You need a pair of white strappy sandals." With that declaration, Sara dragged Allie down the mall to a shoe store, and before she knew what was happening, Allie was trying on shoes. Anything with a high heel was out; she absolutely could not walk in them and couldn't risk breaking an ankle.

They finally settled on some sandals that would probably rub blisters. But they were cute. Cooper didn't even blink at the ridiculous price. Allie hadn't paid that much for all of the shoes in her closet combined.

Cooper seemed to enjoy their shopping outing, which surprised her. Her father had refused to go near a shopping mall, and he'd claimed all men felt the same.

"Sara, do you mind if we make a stop before going back to the B and B?" Cooper asked as they headed back to his car.

"I'm in no hurry."

"How come you didn't ask if I minded?" Allie asked.

"'Cause you're on the payroll."

"I guess that makes you the boss of me," Allie said dryly, but he *was* paying her, so she left it at that. She climbed into the back seat with all the shopping bags—she wasn't up to polite conversation.

"I want to stop by a rental house," Cooper explained. "I can't stay in the B and B indefinitely. The owner said she'd be there all afternoon working on the yard."

Allie was curious what sort of house Cooper would want to live in. Something with a lot of glass and cold stone, probably. So she was surprised when he pulled up in front of a white, two-story frame house with red shutters.

"I know this house," Sara said. "The Mulvaneys live here. You know the Mulvaneys, Allie. Sam runs the Buick dealership. I used to baby-sit their kids."

"Oh, right," she said distractedly. The house was captivating. It had a big palm tree in the front yard and pink petunias growing along the walkway. In fact, it looked disturbingly like the house where Allie had spent her early childhood, before her mom had died.

Her death, like Johnny's, had been expensive. After she was gone, her dad had sold the house, declaring they didn't need such a big place for just the two of them. They'd moved to an apartment near the marina, and eventually they'd given that up, too, and lived on the *Ginnie*, which was a little bit larger than the *Dragonfly*.

She half expected Cooper to eliminate this cozy, family-looking home without even going inside, but he parked and got out.

"You coming?" he asked when she remained in the car.

She opened her door and got out, but she felt a strange sense of dread about entering the house. It was almost as if she was afraid to see how a normal family lived, because she'd been divorced from that reality for so long.

What if she liked what she saw?

It was dangerous to even think about a different way of life. She'd made her choices long ago. Yeah, she'd given up a lot to choose fishing as her way of life. Sometimes she wondered what it would be like to have a garden, or a cat. But spending every day on the water—that was worth an awful lot.

Allie tagged along as Julia Mulvaney showed Cooper around, emphasizing the selling points.

"We're empty nesters now," she explained. "No reason for Jim and me to keep a house this big. But we aren't quite ready to sell it. My daughter says she might like to buy it in a few years, when she and her husband are more established and have kids of their own. I would love to see my grandkids raised in the same house where I raised their mom."

As she'd feared, Allie felt a pang of envy. She had almost nothing from her family. She'd kept a Bible of her mother's, a pocketknife that had belonged to her dad and a few photographs, but that was pretty much it. If she ever had children—and that seemed doubtful—they would never know their grandparents.

She kept expecting Cooper to cut Mrs. Mulvaney off and tell her the house really wasn't his style. But he looked it over thoroughly.

"I'll take it," he said, surprising her. "I'll read the rental agreement tonight and bring it back in the morning. My furniture should arrive next week."

"Great! I'm sure you two will be very happy." She looked not at Sara, who had taken a much more active role in touring the house, but at Allie.

"It's just me," Cooper said hastily.

"I'm not living here," Allie said at the same time. How in the world had this woman gotten the idea Cooper and Allie were a couple?

"Oh, sorry," Mrs. Mulvaney backpedaled. "I just assumed… It's such a family-type of house, I thought…"

"It's only temporary, until I find a place to buy," Cooper said smoothly. But the woman had echoed the same thoughts Allie had. Why would Cooper want to rent here? Any number of rental condos were available with all the conveniences.

Sara had expressed enthusiasm for the house. Maybe he was trying to impress her. Maybe he had a thing for Sara.

Then Allie remembered the way Cooper's eyes had lit up when she'd emerged from the dressing room in the white outfit, and she felt another blush coming on. His gaze had held enough heat to kindle a campfire without matches.

She could deny it all she wanted, tell herself she'd imagined it or that it was impossible, but in her heart, she knew. Cooper wanted her, not Sara.

She wondered if there was any way to use his lust to her advantage, then was ashamed of herself. She had no need to come up with any tricks. She had right on her side.

Anyway, however much he might harbor lustful feelings for her, she had it at least as bad. She hadn't slept a good night's sleep since the morning he'd boarded the *Dragonfly* uninvited. She'd spent way too much time covertly studying him whenever he was within eyesight.

How unfair that the one guy she'd shared chemistry with in a very long time was the one guy in the world she could never be with.

"YOU RENTED A *HOUSE?*" Max's mouth hung open in surprise.

"You'll have to mow the grass," Reece pointed out. "And fix stuff when it goes wrong."

"I can hire people to do that sort of thing, if I find I can't handle it myself." He'd been surprised himself at his decision to rent the Mulvaney home. It was bigger than he needed, and since it was more than forty years old, it would require a lot of maintenance.

He'd lived in Manhattan apartments all his life. He'd never had a lawn, or a backyard, or a tree to climb. He'd never had a bike.

Not that he would go climbing trees or riding bikes now. But he'd been intrigued by the idea of living in a real house. In the end he probably would buy a condo or a townhouse. Max had already found one he liked in a brand-new complex with a golf course and an ocean view.

"It's just for a few months, till I find something to buy. Hey, it was clean, the price was right, and I don't have time to waste apartment hunting. I've got to be ready for a trade show in three days."

Max just shook his head. "Whatever." He lowered his voice. "Did you get our booth bunny outfitted?"

Cooper nodded. "She'll clean up nice." More than nice,

actually. Now that he thought about it, he wasn't so sure he wanted hundreds of men ogling her, even if it did mean traffic for their booth.

Though Allie had been on her own for a long time, he'd come to realize she wasn't particularly sophisticated. She didn't even know how to walk in high heels. His image of her as a femme fatale was wavering. He wondered how well she would handle the inevitable flirtations and outright come-ons she was bound to get.

Of course, if anyone got too familiar and she was unable to discourage the jerk on her own, he'd be there to protect her. What worried him more was, what if she didn't want his protection? She might view an all-expenses paid weekend in Houston as a chance to kick up her heels and have a wild night with some guy she'd never see again.

The possibility made his blood boil.

Oh, Lord, he was in trouble. Yeah, he'd found her attractive from the first minute he'd seen her, her green eyes shooting every kind of warning at him.

But when he'd seen her in those new clothes—nothing even that overtly sexy—something in him had shifted. With a little polish, she would give Heather a run for her money. Even his mother would like her.

Well, maybe not his mother.

He'd booked a suite for himself and Allie at a small, historic hotel near the convention center. It had two bedrooms and two baths, so he wasn't worried that she would object. But he wondered, now, if completely separate rooms wouldn't have been a better idea.

Maybe in separate hotels.

## Chapter Eight

Allie gawked at the lobby of the Hotel Alexander as Cooper registered them. She knew she was acting like the rube she was, but honest to pete she'd never seen anything like this. With its ornate ceilings, inlaid marble floors and chandeliers, it reminded her of something she might have seen on that old show *Dynasty* when she was a kid.

She remained mute as they rode up the gold-gilded elevator to the top floor, and her shock continued as the bellman opened the door to their suite. As she eyed the Oriental rugs and the heavy silk draperies and the coffee table made of some rich, dark wood, her first thought was that this room was fit for a honeymoon—lovers—not antagonistic co-workers on a business trip.

Her second thought was that it must be costing Cooper a fortune.

The bellman carried her small suitcase—borrowed from Miss Greer—to her bedroom and placed it on a luggage rack. He did the same for Cooper's bags. Cooper tipped him and he disappeared.

"What do you think?" Cooper asked, as if her approval meant something. "Nice, huh?"

Allie sank experimentally into a tufted, antique-looking chair. "Uh, yeah. I know you're more accustomed to luxury than me, but aren't you the least bit worried about the bottom line? Trade shows are expensive, and, yes, we'll probably get a few bookings from it, but enough to cover all this?"

"Actually, Remington Industries owns this hotel," Cooper admitted. "I can stay here for free."

"Ah." That explained why he'd been treated like a major VIP the moment he'd walked into the place. "What else does this little family company of yours do?"

He perched on the arm of the sofa and toyed with the tassel on one of half-a-dozen throw pillows. "It owns controlling shares of an amusement park and a commuter airline, a plastics factory, a chain of ice cream parlors—"

"Does that mean we get free ice cream?" she asked hopefully.

"If you want to drive a thousand miles to the northeast."

"Darn, I love ice cream. What else?"

He shrugged. "Real estate development. We started out strictly manufacturing, but over the past fifty years we've diversified—makes us almost recession-proof."

"And you left all that to run a two-bit fishing charter business. I don't get it."

"You're not the only one," he said with a grin. "My parents think I've lost my marbles. But I'm tired of corporate law. It's just the same thing, over and over, trying to cover everyone's butts and protect them from liability, then bailing them out when they get sued.

"Besides," he added, "I've advanced as far as I can. When my father retires as head of the legal department, my older brother will move into that job. I'm pretty much stuck doing what I've been doing for the past eight years. I can't see that as my life for the next thirty years. Can't do it."

Allie couldn't blame him there. "What if you get tired of fishing?" she asked. "It's not an easy life."

"No, I'm beginning to see that I've been a bit idealistic. But it's a challenge. And it doesn't have to be as hard as you're making it. If we bring in enough business, we can hire staff and not get burned out. I have put some thought into this—it's not a lark. I knew as soon as I set foot on the *Dragonfly* that I'd made the right decision."

That was the problem. She'd seen it, too—in his face every time he took the wheel. His love for the sea was real, if nothing else.

She didn't want to feel this way—sympathetic with Cooper. She wanted to keep hating him.

*He hadn't visited Johnny when he was alive,* she reminded herself. *He let his uncle die with no family around him.*

She stood abruptly. "Well, we have a trade show to prepare for. What's next, boss?"

"Insert rod K into slot P—" Allie read from the directions for assembling their rented booth "—being careful to—"

The top canopy suddenly came crashing down on Cooper's head. He let loose with a few select curses while Allie struggled not to laugh.

"—being careful to not let the thing fall on your head?" Cooper finished for her.

The unassembled booth had been waiting for them when they arrived at the convention center. Cooper, who seemed to be a font of endless ready cash, had been willing to pay someone to put it together, but all of the booth company's people were busy.

"I think maybe this requires two sets of hands," Allie said. She was trying to be helpful and cooperative. On the drive down, they had agreed to put aside their legal dispute during the course of the trade show: otherwise they would never accomplish what needed to get done. "I'll get on the ladder and hold this part steady, and you can do the inserting of rods into slots."

When she realized what she'd just said, her face heated up and she cursed her redhead's propensity for blushing.

Cooper flashed her a grin. "Whatever you say."

With a bit more effort, some trial and error, and a minimum of mishaps, the booth came together. It was small and bare bones, but it would get the job done.

Max had put together a video that would continuously play on a wide-screen TV in their booth; with Allie's help he'd tracked down some footage one of the passengers had taken. The video also included interviews with Cooper and Allie as "co-captains," something Allie had agreed to only grudgingly.

Allie had only seen a rough cut of the video. Now, as she watched it in the booth, she was amazed at how professional the final result was. Background music, titles and graphics made all the difference.

"Max spent a couple of years in film school before he decided to go into advertising," Cooper said. He stood beside Allie watching the video.

"He certainly has a lot of creative talent. It never even occurred to me to try something like this."

Max himself showed up later in the day, bringing printed brochures with him. Allie had been consulted on the copy for the brochures. She'd balked at first when the Remingtons wanted to offer gourmet lunch charters and the newly envisioned "champagne starlight" cruises. When the court ruled in her favor and the Remingtons returned to New York with their tails between their legs, how would she fulfill that level of service and luxury on her own?

But Sara, who'd been hanging at the fringes of the planning sessions all week, had offered to help her if needed. And, truth be known, the new ideas excited Allie. She missed the days when she and Johnny used to serve cocktails and a full-service, fancy lunch, and the Remingtons' proposals were a step up even from that.

Max had also brought a banner. The two cousins worked together to hang it, joking and laughing in a way that made Allie mildly jealous. Though she and Cooper weren't arguing, the tension between them was tight as a fishing line pulling in a shark. Yet he wasn't always the arrogant, entitled jerk his first impression might suggest.

She found she enjoyed hearing him laugh, and she listened for it as she pretended to be busy pinning a navy-blue skirt around their booth.

As a lure to get people to visit their booth, they were raffling away three free cruises, which would give them a mailing list.

"Ow!" Damn it, she'd stuck herself with a pin.

Cooper turned from his position on the ladder. "You okay?"

"It's nothing." Though the jab was bad enough that she was bleeding. That would teach her to pay attention to Cooper's butt instead of the task at hand.

She went to her purse to find a tissue, and when that proved fruitless she realized she was going to have to make a trip to the ladies' room.

She turned and nearly mowed down Cooper.

"What happened? You're bleeding."

"I jabbed myself with a pin. It's nothing."

To her surprise he pulled a handkerchief out of his pocket and handed it to her.

"Thank you." She wrapped the hanky around her finger and squeezed to stop the bleeding. "I've never actually seen a person under the age of seventy carry a handkerchief."

"It's an old habit. My mother is big on stuff like that. But see how handy I can be?"

*Handy* wasn't really the word she would use. *Concerned* would be more accurate, which didn't jibe with the man she wanted to believe he was.

"I need a Band-Aid," she said. The injury was minor, and it had already stopped bleeding. But if she didn't cover it, it would sting every time she picked something up.

"Maybe they have a first-aid station somewhere. If not, I saw a drugstore a couple of blocks away."

"It's not worth a special trip." She spied a roll of masking tape and grabbed it. "This'll do for now."

"You'll get an infection and your hand will drop off."

"Cooper, get a grip. It's a tiny pinprick."

"Just don't want anything to happen to my partner."

She got an odd feeling in her chest, hearing the word *partner*. Johnny used to call her that, and it made her feel proud. But coming from Cooper…the feeling was altogether different.

Much as she hated to admit it, she was having fun working on this project with Cooper. She enjoyed brainstorming and sharing problems and responsibilities with someone else. That was one of the things she missed about Johnny—having someone around to bounce ideas off of.

Someone who listened, and actually valued what she

had to say. Someone who cared if she hurt herself, even if it was only a pinprick.

She'd spent far too much time alone the past couple of months, and it was time she faced facts: she couldn't run the fishing charter business by herself. It was too much work for one person, too much responsibility, and it was also a bit dangerous.

What if something happened to her when they were out to sea? What if one of her passengers had an accident or a heart attack? She couldn't take care of a crisis *and* pilot the boat back to shore. And if she were incapacitated, her passengers would have to figure out how to navigate home or summon the Coast Guard.

She needed a partner, and someone like Cooper would be ideal—if they weren't enemies.

Oh, sure, they were cordial now. But if he lost his bid to claim the *Dragonfly*—*when* he lost—he would be furious at her. He would never consent to buy into her business, no matter how much cash he had in his bank account. It was much more likely he would buy his own boat and compete with her.

Besides, he already had partners, two cousins with whom he shared blood and a long history. He had no need for her.

"Is Max staying for the trade show?" Allie asked, needing a distraction from her disturbing thoughts.

"He'll help us get set up in the morning," Cooper answered, "but then he's taking off. He's on a hunt to hire a graphic artist. For this project he had to rely on a freelancer from New York, and the cost was astronomical."

"Too bad he can't hire Jane," Allie said quietly, so Max wouldn't overhear, as she wrapped a piece of masking tape around her smarting finger. "She's very talented. I think she worked as an artist before she got married."

Cooper laughed. "I'm sure that would go over well with Jane's husband." He looked around at their progress. "We're in pretty good shape. Let's knock off for dinner."

"I'm not really hungry," Allie said, though her stomach felt like an empty cave. The truth was, she needed some time away from Cooper to regain perspective. To get angry with him again and remember all the reasons she despised him. "Besides, one of us ought to stay here and keep an eye on things. It would be a shame if that rented TV took a walk."

Later the convention center would be locked up and a security guard would patrol, but right now, the place was chaos.

Cooper actually looked a bit disappointed. "Want us to bring you something back?"

"Sure, a sandwich or something would be great."

She watched the two men walk away, wishing she could go with them but knowing it wasn't a good idea.

While they were gone, she arranged the life-size fish cutouts Max had found somewhere. By the time she was done, schools of smaller fish swimming through a sea of navy-blue satin were chased by bigger fish and even a shark. Their booth was going to look sharp.

An hour later Cooper and Max returned, bearing a take-out bag that smelled heavenly.

"Wow, look at that!" Max stared with exaggerated shock at their booth. "You're really good at this, Allie."

"You think it's okay? Everything's easily movable if you want to change it."

"I wouldn't change a single fin," Cooper added.

His approval warmed her from the inside out. She'd

been hoping they would like her work. She wasn't contributing a dime to this project, and she felt a little guilty that she would be the one to benefit from it. She wanted to do her part however she could.

"Here, this is for you." Cooper handed her a small plastic bag. Inside it she found a box of plastic bandages and a tube of antibiotic cream.

"You act like I've severed a limb," she said with a smile. "But thanks."

It had been a very long time since anyone cared about her well-being. Not even Johnny would have fussed over a small injury. Shoot, when she'd gotten a fishhook stuck in her hand he'd told her to push it through, snip it off, pour some peroxide over it and be done.

She devoured her burger and fries while Cooper and Max put on the finishing touches. At one point Cooper's phone rang, and though she tried not to listen, she gathered the caller was Cooper's mother. He didn't say much, just listened with a pained expression.

It was kind of funny, thinking of Cooper as some woman's little boy.

At ten o'clock they were shooed out so the convention center could lock up.

"Guess I'll see you guys in the morning," Max said as they exited the building and headed in the opposite direction from where Cooper's car was parked.

"Oh, he's not staying at the hotel with us?" The suite was plenty big enough. If Max and Cooper didn't want to share a room—and men were funny about that, even with two huge beds—one of them could sleep on the fold-out sofa in the living area.

"He's made his own arrangements, I guess," Cooper said.

Fabulous. She would be alone in a hotel room with a man who had ignited her fantasies all day long.

A man she couldn't touch with a ten-foot pole.

COOPER HAD NO PRAYER of sleeping. He'd punched his pillow into a hundred different shapes, added and subtracted blankets, even fixed himself a stiff bourbon from the hotel room's minibar. But it was no use.

Images of Allie would not leave him alone.

At least on the boat, he didn't have to look at her all day long. He could distract himself driving the boat or getting a drink for a passenger. But in the close confines of the booth, he'd been unable to avoid watching her.

Thank heavens she'd worn long pants rather than those derelict short-shorts. But the faded denim had hugged her bottom as intimately as a lover, and every time she leaned over, Cooper's mouth went dry. When she reached for something, the shirt rose, giving him a glimpse of her midriff and molding the fabric to her round breasts.

To make matters worse, she'd been pleasant and cooperative the entire day. Under any other circumstances, he would actually like the woman.

He had to remind himself over and over that she was the one who was trying to steal his inheritance. She was the one who'd buffaloed a sick old man into writing a new will.

Of course she was charming and delightful. That was how women stuck it to men.

It didn't seem as if she were deliberately charming him. He was the one who'd suggested they put aside their differences temporarily, so they could survive the weekend and, more important, project an aura of unity to their potential customers.

He'd never imagined cooperation could lead to such personal difficulties.

Suddenly a deafening buzz nearly tossed him out of bed, and he realized it was a fire alarm.

Hell. Seemed like every time he traveled, some joker set off an alarm and he ended up traipsing down umpteen flights of stairs to the lobby, only to discover it was a false alarm.

He climbed out of bed, threw on the shorts and T-shirt he'd planned on wearing for a morning jog, and headed into the living area.

Allie burst from her bedroom. "What's going on? What's happening?"

God Almighty, she had on nothing but a nightgown that was so skimpy she might as well not have bothered.

He looked everywhere but at her. "Jeez, woman, would you put some clothes on?"

"Is there a fire?"

"Probably not." But a recorded voice was blaring from the hallway that they should proceed to emergency exits. "Allie. Put some clothes on." Before he grabbed her and took her right there while the building burned down around them.

She looked down at herself and did that blushing thing she did so well. "Oh. Oh, God."

She darted back into her room and slammed the door. Moments later she reappeared in shorts, T-shirt and flip-flops. She clutched her purse to her chest and looked utterly terrified. "Shouldn't we go?"

"Yes. But don't be scared. It's probably nothing."

"They wouldn't blast us out of bed for nothing." She hurried for the door.

He had to remember that she wasn't a seasoned traveler like he was; this experience could be disconcerting if it was new to you. He followed her out the door. Other people were emerging from their rooms into the hallway, some laughing and making jokes, some clearly irritated.

They all started down the stairwell. No one was scared—until they reached the seventh floor and smelled smoke.

## Chapter Nine

When the group of hotel guests smelled smoke, they got very quiet.

Allie was too terrified to utter a word. This was the stuff her nightmares were made of and one reason she liked being close to the ocean.

They walked down one more flight, but the smoke got thicker and Allie stopped, refusing to go any farther.

"The smoke is probably coming from one of the lower floors," Cooper said. "Smoke rises. We have to keep going down past it."

What he said made sense, but Allie couldn't get her feet to cooperate. She felt as immovable as a hundred-year-old tree.

"Then let's go back up one story," he suggested, "and down the hall to the other stairwell."

She nodded, but she still couldn't move, not until he put his arm around her and gave her a good nudge. She clung to his arm as they walked up past a group of people determined to head down despite the smoke.

When they entered the seventh floor it was clear of smoke. She breathed a small sigh of relief, though she wouldn't truly relax until they were outside on the ground. They made their way down the hall to the opposite side of the hotel.

The second staircase was free from smoke, thank God. Allie ran as fast as she could down the steps, passing other, slower people in her quest.

"Jeez, Allie, you're gonna break your neck," Cooper called from behind her.

She didn't respond, just kept going until they reached the first floor. There, a hotel employee herded everyone out an emergency exit.

As soon as she was outside, she gulped several long breaths of fresh air—well, as fresh as air in downtown Houston ever got. She realized she was hyperventilating and forced herself to slow her breathing before she passed out.

"Are you okay?" Cooper was there beside her, sliding a comforting arm around her shoulders. His arm felt nice there, secure and safe, and she did feel better.

She couldn't talk, but she nodded.

The crowd of people who had evacuated the hotel milled around, dazed and shocked. One poor woman wore nothing but a sheet she'd wrapped around her body, and Allie was glad Cooper had made her get dressed, even if it had taken a few precious seconds to do so.

"Let's get out of this crowd." Cooper took her hand and led her across the street, where they found a place to sit on the edge of a planter.

Allie gazed up at the beautiful old hotel, searching for signs of smoke or flames, but the building appeared perfectly normal—except for all the fire trucks with their flashing lights cutting through the night. The firefighters seemed to be working calmly, not panicking, as if this were a routine job.

"Are you sure you're okay?" Cooper asked again.

"Yes, I'm fine." She forced a smile. "Sorry about the meltdown."

"That's okay. Have you been in a fire before?"

"No. But I have a vivid imagination. And we were so high up, so far from the ground, and that stairwell didn't have any windows…" She shivered.

Cooper rubbed circles on her back. "Come here." He pulled her close to him, and amazingly she let him. It had been so long since she'd let anyone in. No one had comforted her like this since her father died.

Not that she and Johnny hadn't been close. But she always felt like she needed to be strong around him. He'd had his reservations about hiring a woman, so she'd had to present a strong front. She'd never shown him her fears, her vulnerabilities.

It felt so good to lean against Cooper's warm, strong body, to feel his arm around her. She tried not to think too hard about who he really was. Yes, they were involved in a legal battle, and the stakes were very high. But right now it was easy to forget all that. Maybe he was a slick, high-powered lawyer, but his work hadn't beaten all the kindness and compassion out of him.

Or maybe she was just trying to rationalize the warm tingles coursing through her right now. All she knew was that she liked this closeness, and she didn't want it to end.

"So why do you hate lawyers so much?" he asked out of the blue.

She should have known he had an angle. She answered him, anyway. "My uncle was a lawyer. My father died when I was sixteen, and Uncle Daniel was executor of his will. Let's just say, by the time I turned eighteen there was nothing left."

"Jeez. Where was your mother?"

"She died when I was ten."

"Any brothers or sisters?"

"No. Daniel's the only family I have left, and I haven't seen him in ten…"

"…ten years," he finished for her. "Isn't that what you condemned me for?" His tone was merely curious, as if he truly wanted to understand her logic.

"My situation is different. My uncle wants nothing to do with me, and that suits me fine. He's a thief and a liar."

"Hmm." Cooper was silent for a few moments. Then, "Would it surprise you to know that Johnny is the one who refused contact with me?"

"That's not how he told the story." Funny, but just days ago she would have jumped on Cooper accusing him of lying. Now, she felt more as if she'd misunderstood somehow, and she needed more information.

"Oh, I'll admit my father and my other uncles cut off contact initially," he said. "I don't know the details of their feud, but it had something to do with Johnny's drinking.

"Later, when I was grown, I tried to get back in touch with Johnny. I called the marina and left several messages for him. I wrote him five or six letters. He never returned the calls. I sent him a Christmas card every year, and at first he sent one back, but even that stopped.

"I know I should've come down here in person to see him, but I got busy with my life and I figured there would always be time. Johnny wasn't an old man. At least, not in my memory." His voice was thick at the end of his explanation, and Allie wanted to believe he was telling the truth.

But her uncle had told her a lot of pretty stories, too. Stories about how he was taking care of her inheritance, making it grow so she could go to college or buy a house when she turned eighteen.

She didn't want more school or a house. All she wanted was the *Ginnie*, the one place where she could still feel close to her father. But her uncle had put the boat in dry dock against her wishes, insisting a derelict fishing boat was no place for a young girl.

She never saw the boat again.

The day she had sat in a lawyer's office and learned there wasn't enough left of her inheritance to buy a life jacket, much less a boat, she had silently sworn she would never trust anyone again, not unless they earned her trust.

So why did she so badly want to trust Cooper?

They sat on the edge of that planter for about an hour, until a man with a bullhorn announced that the fire had been put out, that it had been confined to only two guest rooms, and it was safe for most of the guests to return to their beds.

"We can check into a different hotel if you want," Cooper said.

"No, I'm staying here. You'll protect me, right?" It was a slightly flirtatious thing for her to say and the words felt alien and a little thrilling on her tongue.

"I wouldn't let anything happen to you. I've tried to hate you, Allie, but I just can't. You're too darn cute." He leaned in and kissed her quickly on the lips. It happened so fast, Allie thought she might have imagined it. But her lips tingled and her whole body thrummed with electricity as they walked across the street and back into the hotel, holding hands.

Allie didn't want it to end. She had no desire to return to her lonely bed, luxurious though it might be, and go to sleep by herself. She wanted to stay up talking with Cooper, sharing bits and pieces of themselves. She wanted to know more about his memories of Johnny and why he had suddenly decided he wanted to chuck a lucrative legal career and become a professional fisherman.

They rode up the elevator in silence, and Allie wondered what he was thinking. Probably that she was a silly girl. "Cute," he'd called her. Did that mean anything? Why couldn't he think she was beautiful or sexy?

Probably because she wasn't either of those things.

He used his key to open the door to their suite. Everything looked just as they'd left it. No telltale smoke lingered in the air.

"We have to get up in three hours," Cooper said.

Allie paused in the living area. "Hardly seems worth going back to bed."

"Do you want a drink?"

"Love one." Did she sound too eager?

Cooper opened the minibar and took stock. "We have Scotch, gin, vodka, and wine. I'm afraid there's no bourbon—I drank that earlier."

That surprised her. "You did? When?" She didn't remember him mixing a cocktail, and he'd headed into his bedroom at the same time she had escaped to hers.

"I couldn't sleep. Too keyed up about the trade show, I guess. I thought a bourbon might relax me."

Funny, she'd had trouble going to sleep, too. "You would think on these huge, soft beds, with all those pillows, we wouldn't have any trouble sleeping."

Oh, dear, maybe she shouldn't have mentioned the big, soft beds, because now that was all she could think about. She'd never made love in a king-size bed before. Hell, she could hardly call the few liaisons she'd had in the past "making love." "Frantic, unfulfilling couplings" was more accurate. Somehow she imagined sex with Cooper would be very different.

"So how about a Scotch and water?" he asked. "Or vodka tonic."

Suddenly liquor didn't sound tempting. She knew what she needed, and he was peering into the mini fridge, giving her an awesome view of his tight butt and muscular legs. A man like him shouldn't be allowed to wear gym shorts.

He straightened and turned to look at her. "Allie?"

Her need must have shone right out of her eyes, because suddenly he had an answering hunger in his.

What would it hurt? If they spent one night together…or two… What difference would it make? Nothing they said or did tonight would change their legal dispute. A judge would decide the outcome, and he would have no knowledge of whether she and Cooper had slept together.

"Cooper…"

That was all she needed to say. He reached her in two long strides, and before she could even take a deep breath to prepare herself, she was in his arms and he was kissing the daylights out of her.

*This* kiss was definitely not in her imagination. His mouth was hot and insistent on hers, his hands were tangled in her hair while hers grasped at his T-shirt, clutching blindly, wanting more of him, more, more…

"Allie, oh, Allie," he whispered against her mouth. "You've driven me completely, utterly insane, and if you don't put a stop to this right now—"

He kissed her again, harder, more demanding, his tongue darting in and out of her mouth. He used one hand to cup her bottom and the other had found her breast, rubbing the nipple with his thumb.

It responded immediately, hardening to a pebble. Her insides turned molten, and she sagged against him, defeated. If he actually hoped she would stop this train, he would be disappointed.

Before she became so boneless that she sank to the floor, he scooped her up and carried her into his bedroom.

Cooper knew what he was about to do was probably the stupidest stunt of his entire life. But he'd lost control of his senses, and right now he hoped he never got them back. He wouldn't, however, compound one stupidity with another.

He laid her on the rumpled bed. "Don't move. Promise me you won't move."

"Where are you—"

He didn't stay to listen. He dashed into his private bathroom and pawed through his shaving kit, praying he hadn't been organized enough to clean this thing out in the past year or so.

Yes! He rushed back to the bedroom relieved to find Allie still sitting there, though she looked a bit bewildered.

When he kissed her again though, it was as if they'd never paused. She came alive in his arms like a wild thing.

Clothes went flying. Cooper couldn't get naked fast enough. He wanted skin against skin. When he got it, it was better than anything he'd imagined. Peaches and cream, kissed golden by the sun. He ran his fingers along her faint tan lines and marveled at how brief her bikini must be.

He pushed her down gently onto the snowy-white sheets, then leaned back so he could admire the effect of seeing Allie tangled in *his* sheets. "You are the most beautiful—"

"No, don't say it." She closed her eyes, as if embarrassed. "'Cute' I can believe. Not beautiful. Don't spoil
this by lying."

She had to be joking. Did she honestly not know how
incredibly gorgeous she was?

He wasn't going to argue with her about it now, though.
There were better things to do than argue. Right now, he
intended to focus on loving her thoroughly, in every way
a man could love a woman without getting arrested.

He kissed her breasts one at a time, circling the nipples
slowly with his tongue as she moaned and wiggled in
semiprotest.

"Oh, my word!"

He chuckled softly as he moved to her other breast.
Meanwhile, his hand explored the fertile territory of her flat
belly, slowly moving down to the soft curls that protected
her feminine secrets.

When he planted a trail of kisses down the center of her
belly and teased her naval with his tongue, he thought she
was going to come unglued.

"Cooper!" she objected.

"What?"

"I'm just—it's just—"

"You don't like it?" He'd never had complaints before.
Then again, a lot of the women he'd dated might have had
an agenda and wouldn't have told him if his lovemaking
wasn't up to their standards.

"I'm overwhelmed, I've never done—oh, shoot, I'm
going to spoil this."

She wasn't a virgin, was she? "You've never…"

"No, I mean, yes, I have, just not so, so… Can we stop
to catch our breath?"

To tell the truth, Cooper had been moving at breakneck speed partly because he wanted her with an intensity he'd never experienced before, but also because he didn't want to give Allie time to catch her breath.

He was afraid she'd change her mind.

But he didn't want to take Allie if she was the slightest bit hesitant. He wanted no regrets. The very nature of their relationship meant they could have no future. No matter how the judge ruled, someone would be ticked off, and that pretty much ruled out anything long-term.

He scooted up next to her, slid an arm behind her and pulled her close. "You're not spoiling anything. I got carried away because, Allie Bateman, you are beautiful. I thought so the first time I saw you, clutching your coffee cup like you were ready to clunk me over the head with it."

That got a little chuckle out of her. "Like I could really hurt you."

"We don't have to do this," he said, though it was painful to consider giving her up, sending her back to her own bed.

"Oh, no! I don't want to stop, Lord no. I just want it to last."

The relief he felt was overpowering. "Don't worry, I'll make it last." He kissed her more gently this time. "And if it doesn't, we'll just do it again."

"Really? You won't roll over and start snoring?"

He laughed. "I don't know what kind of men you're used to, but as long as you're in bed with me, there won't be any snoring going on."

But amusement fled as he set out to deliver on his promises. He kissed and stroked, taking it slow, letting Allie set the pace. He hardly touched her below the waist until she took his hand and dragged it downward.

She parted her legs readily, allowing him full access.

She responded to the lightest of strokes with soft sighs and little gasps, her hands clutching at him wherever she could find purchase.

When he slid a finger inside her, she suddenly cried out and shuddered, and he realized what she meant about wanting it to last. He'd never seen anything as beautiful as Allie in the full throes of ecstasy.

He continued to stroke her until her shudders died down, then he pulled her into his arms and just held her.

"Now you see what I mean."

"What, you think it's a problem? Do you have any idea how it makes me feel, that I can turn you on so quickly? It makes me want to do it all again."

And he did. He kissed and stroked and nibbled until she was writhing again, but this time he quickly sheathed himself and entered her before she climaxed. He moved inside her as slowly as he dared, drawing out their pleasure as long as possible.

"Not yet," he whispered into her ear, going still, then bringing her up to the very brink and slowing again.

By the time he couldn't hold himself back any longer she was almost in tears. And when she came the second time it was even more explosive than the first. Her body clenched around his as she cried out, and his own climax was so…vigorous that he thought he might black out. Every drop of blood that fed his brain had left to take care of more urgent matters.

His body suddenly relaxed, and he slumped on top of her, shifting a bit to the side so he wouldn't crush her.

"Wow," she said.

Now that was the kind of review he liked to hear. "Yeah," he agreed. He'd known just from looking at her that making love with Allie Bateman would be spectacular, but he'd never imagined how much.

"I feel like a boat that's just sailed through a hurricane with all the sails up."

"That's good, I hope."

She laughed. "Oh, yeah." Her face grew pensive. "I think we should do it again, just to prove it wasn't a fluke."

"Have mercy, woman."

"You did promise."

"Give me a few minutes, huh?" He'd created a monster. Fortunately, it was a species of monster he liked.

"Okay, but no snoring."

He figured she'd probably fall right to sleep, but every time he looked at her, her pretty green eyes were wide open and studying him expectantly. Waiting for the snore.

Well, hell, he wasn't about to fulfill *that* expectation.

She began rubbing his chest, almost experimentally, and he guided her hand down where it would do the most good.

"Oh," she said. "Ohh."

He gave her a wicked grin. "I don't believe in false advertising. I said we'd do it all again, and we will."

## Chapter Ten

Allie woke with a start, disoriented and faintly panicked. Was it the fire alarm again?

But, no, it was a cell phone going nuts. A muscular, masculine arm reached past her to turn off the phone, and memories of last night came crashing back into her head.

Oh. My. God. What had she done? She'd slept with the man who was trying to ruin her!

"Morning, gorgeous." He nuzzled her neck and the panic receded slightly. Maybe it wasn't such a bad thing.

"Don't you have to answer the phone?"

"It has an alarm function. I set it for seven."

"Seven?" Judging from the sunlight pouring through cracks in the curtains, she hadn't misheard.

Cooper's nuzzling grew more insistent. "We have plenty of time if you want to—"

Abruptly she sat up. "You might have plenty of time, but it'll take me a while to throw myself together." She jumped out of bed, knowing she was stark naked and that he was watching her, but there was nothing she could do about it.

She quickly gathered up her discarded clothes—Good Lord, how had her panties ended up on the bedpost?—and made a break for it.

She didn't take a full breath until she was safely in her own room.

Time really was short, but that was only an excuse for the cowardly way she'd fled Cooper's bed. She simply hadn't been ready to face the consequences of her actions in the cold morning light. She didn't want to give Cooper the chance to say all those morning-after things men said when they wanted to extricate themselves.

Now that she thought about it, though, he hadn't seemed eager to get rid of her. She touched her neck where he'd been kissing her. Maybe she'd made a mistake.

No, it really was late. And it really would take her a long time to get ready. Aside from the usual showering and dressing, she had to do something with her unruly hair. And, Lord help her, she had to put on makeup and file her nails. No point dressing up in new girlie clothes if the rest of her still looked a tomboy.

Her body felt strange as she let the hot water from the enormous shower's twin sprays beat down on it. Her skin was sensitive in a way it never had been before. It was almost like she had a brand-new body, and as she soaped herself up she couldn't help remembering all the places Cooper had kissed her, touched her.

All alone in her shower, her nipples hardened and she blushed.

She used the built-in blow-dryer to straighten her hair, making it a little easier to style. She thought about leaving it loose—for a change it wasn't all over the place. But she decided it would just get in her way, so she pulled it back in a loose braid and pulled a few strands loose to frame her face. In the bathroom's humidity, they started curling again.

Makeup was even more of a challenge. She'd never worn

makeup on a regular basis and had never excelled at applying it. She had to do her eyeliner three times before she got it straight. She managed to get mascara in her hair, and her first attempt at eyeshadow was so heavy-handed that she had to wipe it off with a wet washcloth and start over.

But in the end, she was pleased with the results. As she studied her reflection in the full-length mirror on the back of the door, she felt she was looking at a different person. An Allie Bateman clone who lived an altogether different life from her own.

*This* Allie wore beautiful clothes, stayed in luxury hotels, and had sex with handsome and completely unsuitable men.

When she emerged from her room she got another surprise. A waiter was just leaving; he'd set up a table for two near the window, and the delectable scents of bacon and coffee tickled her nose.

Cooper turned after closing the door and greeted her with a smile. In a pressed Hawaiian shirt, baggy khakis and Top-Siders, he looked even more delicious than the breakfast that no doubt awaited her. Still rather neat, but inching toward Jimmy Buffet casual.

"You look fantastic."

The way he was looking at her, like he wanted to devour her on the spot, made her *feel* fantastic. "Thank you. You ordered breakfast?"

"Since you felt pressed for time, I thought this would be faster. I wasn't sure what you wanted so I ordered a little bit of everything."

She was so hungry she could *eat* a little of everything. Maybe even a lot of everything. When she inspected the contents of the covered plates on the rolling cart next to their table, she found eggs, biscuits, pancakes, waffles, French toast, sausage and bacon.

"You weren't kidding," she said. "I would love waffles."

"They're all yours." He served them both, poured them orange juice and coffee.

She felt like a princess. It was sweet of him to go to all this trouble and expense just so she wouldn't feel rushed. She'd ogled the prices on the room service menu. He might be getting the room for free, but she bet he had to pay for the food. This spread probably set him back seventy-five dollars.

She'd never known what it was like to have disposable income. She'd never gone hungry, and her father had earned enough that she had all the necessities. Later, when she was earning her own paycheck, she socked away every spare penny with the idea of buying her own boat.

But luxuries had never been a part of her life, and she felt a little strange letting Cooper provide them for her. But as she crunched down on the perfectly cooked waffle topped with fresh strawberries and whipped cream, she realized she could get used to this.

*Hah. Dream on, girl.* This was a once-in-a-lifetime treat for her—all of it, including the mind-blowing lovemaking.

"I don't mean to rush you," Cooper said, "but we probably should get a move on. We have a lot of last-minute adjustments to make before the convention center doors open."

"Oh. Right." She was the one who'd flown out of bed in a panic about the time, and here she was woolgathering.

THE CONVENTION CENTER was a beehive of frenzied activity as everyone hustled to be ready by ten o'clock. Allie fussed with the satin booth skirt, evening out the pleats, and Cooper set out an antique fisherman's basket to hold the entries for their drawing, as well as the blank entry forms and pens.

Max showed up at ten minutes to ten with his last contribution—give-away key chains with little dolphins printed with *Remington Charters, Port Clara, Texas* and a phone number—not hers, she noticed.

"Whose phone number is this?" she asked.

"My cell phone," Cooper answered. At her frown he added, "Don't worry. If you end up with the boat, I'll refer any potential customers straight back to you."

She eyed the stack of glossy brochures suspiciously. It hadn't occurred to her to check the phone number. She picked up one off the stack and flipped it over. It listed her number, not his.

Cooper smirked at her.

"Very fair-minded of you," she said. "I'll extend the same courtesy."

"I'll leave you guys to it," Max announced. "I'm supposed to meet with some artists." He took off.

"Yeah," Cooper grumbled, "and if he doesn't hire them, he'll take them to bed."

"He's a real Romeo, huh?"

"It's not his fault. The women offer."

"Jane didn't offer, I'm pretty sure of that."

Cooper grinned. "Okay, so it's partly Max's fault. He can't help himself."

"And what about you?"

"I couldn't help myself last night, that was for sure." The look he gave her was so hot she was ready to forget the trade show and go back to bed. But then the convention center doors opened and potential customers streamed in.

Allie put on her professional face and prepared to sell the heck out of herself and her business.

Traffic was thin the first couple of hours. Allie struck up a conversation with the woman in the exhibit next door, which was promoting a fancy day spa in the Hill Country. The woman was bored and offered to paint Allie's nails for free.

"Your nails are a really nice shape," the woman commented as she applied red polish. Her name was Candy, which seemed appropriate given that she looked like a pop star. "You should grow them out a little."

"I wouldn't be able to work with long nails." Allie could just imagine trying to repair the boat's engine or bait a fishhook with long claws.

"So is the man working with you your husband?"

Allie laughed. "Oh, Lord, no! He's someone I've been forced to work with for a short while, but very soon he'll be out of my life." That thought didn't bring her as much satisfaction as it should have. Though she was terrified of losing the *Dragonfly,* Cooper's abrupt entry into her life had given it a certain sense of excitement, like she'd awakened from a long sleep.

Maybe she'd been depressed. She had been doing the bare minimum to get by and no more, taking no real pleasure in her work. She probably would have come out of it eventually as the sting of losing Johnny lessened, but Cooper Remington had jolted her out of it sooner rather than later.

"So he's unattached?" Candy asked, studying Cooper so intently she blobbed red polish across Allie's knuckle. "Oops, sorry." She quickly wiped up the mishap.

"Trust me, you don't want to mess with him. He's trouble."

"I like trouble."

Allie didn't doubt it. "He's a lawyer."

Rather than dampening Candy's interest, that tidbit made her nose twitch like that of a bird dog on the scent of quail. "No kidding. Okay, we're done here. Put your hands under this drying lamp for a few minutes so you don't smudge. I've just *got* to go check out this trouble-some lawyer."

"Your funeral." But as Candy sashayed out of the spa's booth, Allie felt distinctly uneasy. Obviously two hours of mindless passion didn't qualify her to make claims on Cooper. But that didn't mean she wanted to watch as he made another conquest.

She wasn't sure who she felt sorrier for—Candy, falling victim to Cooper's irresistible nature, or Cooper, becoming the target of an obvious man-hunter. Maybe they deserved each other.

Another woman from the spa booth sat down beside Allie. Two other spa employees—all of them dressed in white lab coats open to reveal tight, low-cut shirts and miniskirts—were working on potential customers, giving a chair massage to one and putting makeup on another.

"Hey, thanks for coming over," the woman said. "Seems to have broken the ice. We have a line forming."

"No charge. My nails have never looked this pretty."

"Candy's good. She's also good with men, so if you have any claim on that delicious guy in your booth—"

"No, no claim." She knew her voice was brittle. She couldn't resist peeking over her shoulder at Cooper and Candy. The two of them were talking and smiling. Cooper was apparently getting Candy signed up for a chance to win a free cruise.

Candy would win over Allie's dead body.

The ferocity of her thoughts frightened her a bit. Maybe she better remove herself before she said or did something fatally stupid.

"My nails are dry. I think I'll go walk around a bit." Maybe if she drew a few customers into the booth, they would get a line, too. She walked up to her own booth, grabbed a stack of brochures without even looking at Cooper and Candy, and set off down the aisle to "work the crowd." She had no idea how that was really done, since she'd never done it and she wasn't the world's most social animal, but she gave it a shot.

She saw two women standing in the middle of the aisle gazing around, apparently trying to decide where to go next. Allie strode up to them with her best smile, holding out one of the brochures.

"Hi, I'm Captain Allie Bateman of Remington Charters out of Port Clara. Would you like to win a free deep-sea fishing adventure for four?" she asked brightly.

"We don't fish," one of the women said dismissively.

Allie refused to be discouraged. "I can teach you. Don't you love fresh red snapper, cooked over the grill with a bit of butter, garlic and tarragon? And I bet your husbands or boyfriends love to fish. Kids love it, too. Do you have kids?"

One of the women took the brochure. "I have a teenage son. He doesn't love anything."

"Get him out on the ocean in the fresh air, away from his computer, and I bet he'd have a blast. The Remington Charters booth is just at the end of this aisle on the left. We're giving away three free cruises."

"Okay, we'll sign up."

As the two women took off, Allie congratulated herself. Cooper could sit around in the booth and flirt if he wanted to; she would show him how to get customers.

She tried a similar approach with men, and it worked even better because lots of them already liked to fish. Husband-wife couples were a little more difficult, especially when the wives caught the husbands looking at Allie's chest, which they invariably did. One woman declared she wouldn't let her husband sail on any boat where Allie was sailing, too. But many of them were interested, especially the ones who had kids too old for Disneyland and too young for a Carnival Cruise.

By the time she made a complete circuit around the convention center floor, she'd given away a thick stack of brochures and there was quite a crowd gathered around the booth. Some were signing up for the drawing, some were watching the video and some were listening raptly to Cooper wax enthusiastic about fishing in the Gulf of Mexico. She had to admit, his flair for the dramatic— probably honed through courtroom performances—made a trip with Remington Charters sound like the greatest adventure since Indiana Jones went looking for the lost ark.

Allie worked her way up to the booth. "Miss me?"

"Where have you been?" he asked under his breath, sounding mildly annoyed. "We're suddenly swamped."

"We're swamped because I've been out hustling," she said. "I'll stay here and keep an eye on things if you want to take a break. Maybe go next door and hang out with Candy?"

He gave her a blank look. "Candy?"

"The blonde from next door?" Allie nodded toward the spa booth.

"Oh, her." He looked puzzled for a moment longer, then a slow grin spread across his face. "Jealous?"

"Of course I'm not jealous!" she sputtered. "Just because we… I mean, I don't have any reason to… That's ridiculous." As he seemed to take more and more enjoyment from her indignant response, she realized she was just digging her grave deeper, so she clamped her mouth closed.

He laughed. "You are jealous."

Denials were useless. She sighed. "Would anyone like a free key chain?" she asked the small crowd. "When you squeeze the dolphin his eyes light up." All of the women with small children jumped at the dolphin key chains. Cooper, still smiling, took his own stack of brochures and went to work on the convention floor. Shortly after, a small flurry of women approached the booth. Wouldn't they be surprised if they booked cruises for a few weeks later in the season and arrived to find no sign of Cooper?

They stayed busy the rest of the day with a constant stream of potential customers, some of them seriously interested. By the end of the day Allie's feet were killing her, her throat was sore and her hair was coming loose from its moorings. But the fishing basket was stuffed with entries, which meant lots of names to add to their mailing list, and they'd booked seven reservations for future cruises with deposits paid.

Allie's cell phone had started ringing, too. Apparently some people who hadn't actually made it to the booth had looked at the brochure later and had been intrigued enough to ask questions.

When the last of the convention attendees were shuttled out of the building, Allie collapsed into a chair. "Just shoot me now. That was the hardest work I've ever done."

Cooper looked exceedingly pleased with himself. "And just think, tomorrow we get to do it all again."

"Do you think someone could bring a stretcher to carry me back to the hotel? My shoes are rubbing blisters."

"I just bought you a whole box of Band-Aids."

"They're back at the hotel."

Cooper, still seemingly full of energy, was packing and straightening up the booth. "I'll get the car and pick you up at the exit so you don't have to walk so far."

"I'd appreciate it."

"You'll have a couple of hours to rest and put your feet up before the party."

Allie sat up straighter. "Party? What party?"

"We've been invited to a cocktail party hosted by the Gulf Coast Yacht Club."

Allie yawned. "You'll have to go without me. The only thing on my agenda this evening is a long, hot bath and an early bedtime." She didn't want to elaborate on exactly why she hadn't gotten enough sleep last night, because she was kind of hoping Cooper had forgotten about it.

"You have to go," he said. "The members of this club are exactly the sort of customers we want—very wealthy and already into boats."

"If they already own boats, why would they want to charter ours? I mean, mine." She couldn't believe she'd slipped like that.

"Because we don't just offer a boat. We provide them with the whole package—the equipment, the bait, the fish-cleaning."

"So what do you need me for? Clearly you can talk up Remington Charters without my help."

"Trust me, you need to be there. You're part of the package."

"Oh, so you want the men to ogle my breasts while you sell them on the business? Is that it?"

Cooper's face clouded. "No, Allie, that is not it. You are

the best fishing guide in Port Clara, and possibly the whole Texas Gulf Coast. Everybody agrees you can find the fish, you know what bait to use. Yeah, the men like to look at you. But the moment you open your mouth and start talking fishing, they're mesmerized.

"Maybe it escaped your attention," he concluded, "but we work well as a team."

She forced herself to relax. Yes, she had noticed it. He was strong in areas where she was weak, and vice versa. "I'm sure the party would be loads of fun and good for business, but I don't have anything appropriate to wear to a cocktail party."

"What about the dress?" His voice went slightly husky, and his eyes grew bright and hot.

"I didn't bring it."

"Sure, you did. Go look in your suitcase."

## Chapter Eleven

Cooper had just managed to extricate himself from another uncomfortable phone call from his mother when Allie emerged from her room wearing the halter dress, and he nearly swallowed his tongue. She'd swept her hair up on top of her head, secured with a gold clip, and her makeup was more dramatic than it had been during the day.

"Wow. You look like a dream."

She rolled her eyes. "Yeah, thanks."

Okay, so she wasn't happy that he'd bought the dress despite her veto. She'd get over it. "Has no one ever taught you how to take a compliment? The correct response is, 'Thank you.' Perhaps adding, 'You look nice, too.'"

She seemed to see him for the first time, eyeing him up and down. She cocked her head to one side. "You do look nice. No, *nice* isn't the right word. Fantastic. Movie star-ish. Godlike. But you must be used to hearing that about yourself. I'm not. I know I'm not beautiful, so when you say that I am, it makes me suspicious, that's all."

"Suspicious that I want something from you?"

"Exactly."

He walked slowly toward her, his gaze focused on her full lips. "I do want something from you. But I don't need to resort to false flattery. You are beautiful, and I refuse to believe no one has told you that before."

As he drew even closer, her eyes got that deer-in-headlights look about them. "N-no one I'd trust."

He pushed her gently against the wall. She tried to evade his kiss, but he held her chin between his fingers and found his mark, kissing her sweet-glossed lips until he had her full attention. She smelled like the hotel bubble bath, which didn't surprise him since she'd soaked for a good hour after they returned to their suite. The skin of her bare shoulders was smooth as a river stone but a lot softer and warmer.

Allie made a small noise of protest in the back of her throat, and he reluctantly dragged his mouth from hers. "You're beautiful."

"I'm not—"

He cut her off with another kiss, this time cupping one breast in his hand. She had the most incredible breasts in the universe. "You're beautiful," he said again. "Are you questioning my judgment and taste?"

"But you just—"

"Yes, I want to take you to bed. Do you think I take ugly women to bed?"

That made her laugh. "Probably not as a rule."

"Okay, then."

"So looks are the only criteria?" she asked.

"That is another argument entirely, and I'm not prepared to educate you on my dating and bedding criteria. Suffice it to say I want to take you to bed, and not only because you're beautiful."

"What other reason is there?" she asked as he kissed her neck.

"It might surprise you to know that I'm attracted to women who have both beauty and brains. And passion. And a sense of humor. If all I cared about was looks, I could have had Candy."

Allie stiffened in his arms. "It's not too late."

"You're being deliberately obtuse. I want you. Not Candy."

She put her arm around his neck and stared into his eyes, her moist lips slightly parted, her gaze heavy-lidded. "Then let's ditch the party."

"Duty before pleasure, my lovely. But now we have something to look forward to, yes?"

He kissed her one more time, for good measure, and this time she gave as good as she got. He released her only reluctantly. "You might want to touch up your lipstick."

"You might also."

THE YACHT CLUB PARTY was on the top floor of one of Houston's most elegant hotels, complete with crystal chandeliers and roaming, tuxedoed wait staff bearing trays of champagne and caviar hors d'oeuvres. Such events were old hat to Cooper, but not Allie. He enjoyed watching her face as she took it all in, her eyes as wide as a child's on Christmas morning.

"You might want to close your mouth before the flies get in," he whispered in her ear. He'd slid an arm around her waist the moment they'd stepped off the elevator and he intended to keep her by his side. If any predatory men at this party thought they could make a meal of Allie, he would be sure they knew she was his.

No, not his. He suspected Allie would never belong to

any man, especially not him. But so long as they were partners, she was under his protection and no one was going to take advantage of her.

Allie clamped her mouth closed. "I'm underdressed."

She was the most beautiful woman in the room, but he'd told her that sort of thing enough for one night. "You look fine." He snagged two glasses of champagne and handed one to Allie.

She took an experimental sip. "Wow."

"This definitely isn't the stuff you can buy for $5.99 a bottle at the corner liquor store," he agreed after his own taste.

"I want to try the snacks," she said. "I'm guessing they're something special, too." She looked around. "No one else is eating. Maybe rich people think it's gauche to actually eat at a party."

He wasn't sure if the "aw shucks" act was real, or if she was subtly taking a dig at him, reminding him of the difference in their backgrounds. "You can eat the snacks and no one will think you're gauche as long as you take small bites and don't stuff extras down your cleavage for later."

"No need for that. I'm so hungry I'll probably eat everything in sight." Despite her threat, she got herself a plate from a buffet line, then only put two small canapés on it. She tasted one, then another, looking thoughtful.

"What's the verdict?" he asked.

"I'll stick to the champagne," she said. "I can make better appetizers than these."

"Really?" Again, he considered what a boon it would be if Allie could work for him—long-term, not just until the *Dragonfly* was back in the water.

She shrugged. "If I can get the right ingredients and I have time."

"What about cooking facilities?" he asked. "Are the *Dragonfly*'s adequate for fancy cooking?"

Another shrug. "There's an oven, a grill and a cooktop, a few pans and utensils. A gourmet seven-course meal is beyond my capabilities, but I can do better than cold cuts. Why are you asking me this? 'Cause much as I love to cook, you aren't demoting me to galley slave."

"Don't get all defensive on me. I'm just wondering what is and isn't possible. Our brochures do say something about gourmet food."

"And I did caution you about making excessive promises."

They couldn't continue the argument because Jim Jameson, president of the yacht club, had spotted Cooper and was making a beeline for him. Stuck to his arm was an obvious trophy wife, maybe thirty years old to his fifty-plus.

"Remington!" he bellowed. "Glad you could make it. And this must be your girl."

Cooper felt Allie stiffen beside him even as she extended a hand toward the other man.

"I'm Allie Bateman, Cooper's partner," she corrected gently.

Jim smiled slyly as he took Allie's hand and, rather than shaking it, brought it to his lips. "Oh, I get it. You all have one of those modern arrangements. Don't want to be tied down, eh?"

Allie snatched her hand back, her green eyes sparkling dangerously. "No, Mr. Jameson, I don't believe you do get it. Cooper and I are business partners. I'm not his wife or girlfriend or plaything."

Cooper cringed inwardly. Although it was refreshing to see Allie go off on someone besides Cooper for a change, Jim Jameson wasn't someone she should be insulting. The man was powerful, a millionaire half-a-dozen times over, and he could open doors for them.

Thankfully, Jim didn't seem to be easily offended. "Of course, of course," he said. "I didn't mean to imply anything unseemly. You two come with me, there's people I want you to meet." He offered Allie his arm, and she reluctantly took it, giving Cooper an annoyed eye roll over her shoulder as she and Jim walked off, leading the way. Cooper gave his arm to the trophy wife and followed.

The next few minutes were given over to meeting and greeting some of the Gulf Coast Yacht Club's elite. Once Allie relaxed a bit, she became the belle of the ball. A few of the men had heard of her, as females running fishing charters were pretty rare. She didn't seem ill at ease, even when confronted by wives dripping in diamonds who sensed her lack of sophistication and, perhaps feeling threatened by her youth and beauty, tried to put her down.

But she didn't let them get to her. Her small-town ways were charming, and Cooper found himself silently cheering her on as she made friends of the women and impressed the men with her knowledge of sailing and fishing.

She managed to subtly turn away flirtations without ruffling any feathers, which left Cooper feeling more relieved than he ought to. If she met some billionaire playboy who could set her up on her own boat, it would soften the blow of losing the *Dragonfly*—if she did lose. Maybe she'd even release her claim on the boat. But the thought of Allie in the arms of another man made his blood turn to steam.

He never should have slept with her. Now that he had, though, it was like Pandora's box. He couldn't put the lid back on.

Even as these thoughts chased through his head, Cooper did his best corporate networking, exchanging his newly printed business cards with other boat owners. As Allie had pointed out, people who owned yachts probably weren't their target customers. But they might very well have friends who were.

By ten o'clock the party was in full swing, but Allie looked tired and Cooper took pity on her. They had another full day ahead of them. He extricated her from a group of younger women she appeared to be bonding with; they said a few goodbyes and slipped out.

"Thank God," she said, leaning against the elevator wall and closing her eyes. "That was exhausting."

"You didn't enjoy it?"

She shrugged one delicate shoulder. "I'm not really a party girl. I guess I prefer my own company to just about anyone else's."

"Not too many people can say that."

"A lot of people are scared to be alone with themselves, so they fill every spare minute with parties and drinking, TV, talking on the phone, shopping, cruising the Internet. But give me a quiet morning anchored in a deserted cove, just me and the ocean and sky and maybe a few seabirds. That's when you really find out who you are."

"You paint a pretty picture. Only one problem with it."

She opened her eyes to look at him. "What's that?"

"No man in it."

"I don't need a man."

"Last night says you do."

She backed away from him. "Last night was…unusual."

"That's one way to put it."

The elevator doors opened onto the hotel lobby and

Allie scurried out. She refused to meet his gaze as they waited under the hotel canopy for the valet to bring around his car. She continued to look uncomfortable as he drove the few blocks back to their own hotel.

All day he'd been looking forward to tonight, when he could have Allie all to himself again, naked and burning with passion in his bed. But her current attitude didn't bode well for his plans.

It seemed she was having second thoughts.

The valet opened her door, and she stepped out and thanked him with a dazzling smile. She could have been a princess instead of a tomboy boat captain. She walked ahead of him toward the hotel's revolving door, and he noticed the light dusting of freckles on her shoulders.

The curve of her bare back made his mouth go dry.

Nothing more was said until he unlocked the door to their suite.

"Well, we've got a long day ahead of us," Allie said with false brightness. "I'm going to bed."

"Whoa, wait a minute."

She skidded to a stop. "What?"

"Aren't you forgetting something? Didn't we go to the party looking forward to when it was over?"

"You caught me in a weak moment. You *know* us having sex is a bad idea."

He sighed. "If that's how you feel. We could at least sit down and unwind. Maybe have a glass of wine and talk about our strategy for tomorrow."

"Talk? You really want to talk?"

Amazingly, if they couldn't go straight to bed— together—he did want to talk. Allie was one woman whose company he didn't find tedious, who didn't talk endlessly about shopping and TV shows he didn't watch and the love lives of people he didn't know and what her latest body-mass-index reading was at the health club.

"What I really want is to take you to bed and make love to you all night. But I get the distinct feeling that's not in the cards."

Her shoulders slumped in defeat and she turned to face him. "Cooper, please. I don't want to turn you down. In fact, I'm not sure I can. You're too persuasive. So could you just cut me some slack and not push it?"

He sighed again, louder this time. If she'd played coy, he might have enjoyed the challenge of chasing her. But he couldn't now, not when she looked like she was about to cry.

"Okay," he said agreeably, as if it didn't matter that much to him. "I'd still like a glass of wine to relax. How about you?"

She flashed him a cautious smile. "Sure."

When they were settled comfortably in the living area— him in a chair, her on the sofa—with cold glasses of Chablis from the minibar, Cooper finally felt the tension seeping out of his muscles.

"Don't worry, I intend to honor your wishes," he said. "But I would like to know why you don't want to spend the night with me."

"Cooper. Surely you don't need me to explain this to you. We are technically enemies who have called a temporary truce. There's no future in you and me. Yes, I've been alone for a while, but I'm not desperate enough to compound last night's mistake with more of the same."

He lifted his glass to her. "Thank you for explaining all that to me. But I have never once thought of you as desperate." In fact, *he* was the desperate one. Because the longer he sat there looking at but not touching Allie, the more he wanted her.

It shouldn't matter. Why did it matter?

"Do you regret last night?" he asked her.

She looked down. "Last night we were in unusual circumstances."

"You didn't answer my question."

After a moment she looked back at him, holding his gaze so long that he finally had to look away. "No," she said. "I don't regret it. We were carried away, and I can forgive myself for that. Once."

"More than once, if memory serves."

He could have sworn a bit of fire flared in her green eyes.

"Don't get technical on me."

If he set down his wine, stood, walked the three steps that separated them and pulled her out of that chair and into his arms, would she still deny him? He had a feeling the answer was no. But he'd told her he wouldn't push, and if he went back on his word he would just confirm every stereotype she harbored about dishonest, conniving, self-serving lawyers in general and him in particular. He had a responsibility to uphold the image of lawyers everywhere.

Right.

He gulped the rest of his wine in two swallows. Might as well face it, nothing was going to cool his ardor while Allie was within his range of vision wearing *that* dress. He wasn't sure whether to thank Sara or curse her for convincing him to buy it even though Allie had nixed it.

Standing up, he set down his glass. "Guess it's good night, then. I'll order breakfast for about seven."

She nodded and cleared her throat.

He turned, took two steps, then stopped. Had Allie's

eyes been shiny with tears? Surely not. But his feet remained rooted to the spot. He couldn't bear it if he'd made her cry.

Slowly he peeked at her over his shoulder. She had her head down, her hands clasped in her lap, her breasts rising and falling in a too-quick rhythm to be natural breathing.

Damn it.

He was at her side and down on one knee in two seconds. "Allie, baby, what's wrong?"

"N-nothing. Go away."

"I won't. Did I say something wrong?"

She took a deep, broken breath. "N-no. You said everything right. You did exactly what I asked you to do."

"Then what's the problem?"

"The problem…" She looked up at him, her eyes swimming in tears. "The problem is me. I'm weak and an idiot to boot."

"You're the strongest woman I've ever met."

"But not the smartest! Because secretly I was hoping you would make it impossible for me to say no."

## Chapter Twelve

Cooper was looking at Allie like he wanted to devour her in one bite.

"Could you just leave me with whatever shreds of dignity I have left, please?" She didn't like begging, but she was in desperate trouble here. He was within touching distance. In fact, he was touching her, smoothing her hair off her face, tucking a strand behind her ear.

Did he have to be so tender? Life would be so much easier if he was a complete jerk.

"You're killing me here, Allie. I want you, you know that. But I won't have you blaming me for pushing or taking advantage. I know I've brought a lot of trouble into your life, and for that I apologize. But I won't apologize or feel bad about making love to you.

"So I'm going to stand up and walk into my room. I hope you'll follow. But that's entirely up to you. Are we clear on that?"

"You lawyers talk too damn much." She cupped his jaw in her hand and kissed him hard enough to make him go cross-eyed. She was beyond caring who had manipulated whom. Her mind was too filled with the smell and taste of him, the feel of his hands all over her, the sound of his low moans of pleasure as she rediscovered territory she'd charted the previous night.

She nearly ripped his shirt getting it off him, and she mentally thanked him for buying the halter dress because it was so easy to take off. Cooper gave the bow at the back of her neck one tug, and the dress floated to the floor.

They never even made it to the bedroom. Cooper somehow had a condom handy, and they made love right there on the sofa. It happened in a blinding flash, yet at the same time Allie felt suspended in time as he filled her head with soft yet urgent endearments, and filled her body with himself.

Allie couldn't have stopped any more than she could halt her breathing.

She felt her body tingle in a way she recognized, and she held her breath trying to prolong the exquisite feelings. Then her climax washed over her. She felt it in every cell of her body, down to her fingernails and the tips of her hair.

Cooper cried out in triumph as he found his own release, and they held each other for several long minutes. Allie was afraid to move, knowing she would break the spell holding them still on this plateau of pure sensation.

When the air conditioning kicked on, Allie shivered and Cooper stirred, shifting to a slightly more comfortable position on the sofa and pulling her against him. He sighed contentedly.

"Cooper—"

"Allie—"

They both stopped. Allie laughed nervously and Cooper barreled ahead. "Allie, please, please don't start in with how big a mistake this is. There's just no point."

"I was only going to suggest we move to your bed," she

said in a slightly injured tone. She wouldn't regret this. She couldn't. Already she knew it would be painful when they resumed their antagonistic roles, but pain wasn't exactly something new to her.

He smiled and kissed her on the forehead. She couldn't remember ever seeing his face so boyish and unguarded. "Good idea."

They fell asleep wrapped in each other's embrace, but later Allie awoke to the delicious sensation of Cooper kissing her neck. He didn't stop there, however. He kissed her all over, *everywhere*, places she'd never imagined being kissed. He worshiped her body in a way that made her believe he enjoyed it as much as she did, and they made love again, this time in slow motion, pausing to appreciate every nuance of feeling, every touch, every breath, every whisper of the silky sheets.

Allie knew it was the last time. Tomorrow, after the trade show, they would pack up and drive back to Port Clara, back to the real world where a court battle awaited them.

When she was sure he was asleep, she turned her face into the feather pillow and cried for something that could never be.

WHEN COOPER EASED INTO wakefulness, it was still dark out. He wondered what had awakened him, then remembered the beautiful woman in his bed and realized he'd awakened many times that night, each time reaching out to make sure she was still there.

He briefly considered tying her to the bed to prevent a repeat of yesterday morning when she'd fled him in a panic, then smiled into the darkness at the mental picture of how furious she would be if he tried anything like that, even as a joke.

But his smile faded as he realized that nothing he could do would hold Allie. No matter what she'd said last night, she would regret this. Because Allie Bateman wasn't a no-strings-sex kind of woman.

She might not know it, but Allie was a long-term, ring-on-her-finger, forever kind of woman. And he was the last person with whom she could possibly have forever.

As he lay there in the growing dawn light, perhaps still half-asleep and unguarded, a strange thought took hold of him. At first he dismissed it as ridiculous, but the thought kept coming back.

Maybe he needed to take a novel approach to the problem of Allie and her claim on Johnny's boat. Yes, he was used to approaching problems from a win-lose per-spective. The law had always been his comfort, something in black and white that, when skillfully interpreted, solved all dilemmas. He pursued legal avenues until he came out on top, or didn't, though usually he did because he'd never been one to squander resources on iffy legal battles.

Allie, however, required some thinking outside the box. How could they both win? How could they each get what they wanted and remain friends—or lovers?

Allie had already rejected a cash settlement. But what if he made her a different kind of offer?

Though it was tempting to wake her up and tell her what he was thinking right away, he decided to let her sleep while he chewed on this new, better solution. He thought about it while he showered and shaved, and while he dressed in a wild Hawaiian shirt he'd borrowed from Max knowing it would make Allie smile. If she wanted him to be a "Mar-garitaville" kind of guy, he'd give it to her in spades.

Breakfast had just arrived when she woke up. He saw

her standing in the doorway to his bedroom, wrapped in his terry cloth robe, looking adorably rumpled and sleepy.

"Why didn't you wake me?" she asked as soon as the waiter had gone.

"You looked so peaceful, so I thought I'd let you get an extra hour of sleep."

"Well, you did keep me up late," she said with a saucy toss of her head.

As if he needed reminding of last night. "Come sit down. We don't have to rush today, since everything is already set up." He poured her coffee and orange juice and uncovered all the dishes.

"Do you eat like this every day?" she asked as she scooped up a small portion of scrambled eggs and added one strip of bacon and one toast triangle.

"Most days."

"If I ate like this all the time, pretty soon I wouldn't fit through the *Dragonfly*'s hatch."

"I just burn it off, I guess." But maybe he should start considering his health. He'd never thought much about the future before, figuring it would take care of itself. But he wanted to live a long time. Now that he had a future really worth living, he wanted to make it last.

He added a healthy portion of fresh fruit to his plate. "So, speaking of the *Dragonfly,* I've been thinking."

Her fork stopped midway to her mouth, and she looked up warily. "Cooper, haven't we done enough thinking? I mean, we've already launched several of your ideas—different kinds of cruises, new ways of marketing. Shouldn't we see if all this newfangled stuff works before we start even more? Maybe you can afford to lose money on high-risk ideas, but I can't."

"I couldn't agree more, and I don't intend for you to bear more risk than you can withstand. This is something a little different."

"Okay. Shoot."

"You and I work pretty well together, don't you agree?"

She had to think about it for a few moments. "When we're not fighting, yeah. You're pretty easy to work for, and you've certainly shouldered your fair share of responsibilities."

"If we didn't have this legal problem hanging over our heads, we would be compatible partners. Right?"

She took a long sip of her coffee, watching him carefully over the rim of her cup. "What are you getting at?"

"Say the judge awards you the boat. You'll have to hire someone to help you handle all the cruises we're booking. The same is true of me—because frankly, though my cousins are enthusiastic about the boat, Reece gets seasick and Max is going to be too busy with his new ad agency to help me much.

"But if you and I continue our partnership indefinitely, we can share the work and the profits."

"So what you're thinking," she said slowly, "is that once the fishing business is legally yours, I'll be your employee. Not interested." She took a bite of toast and chewed it furiously, staring out the window.

"That's not what I meant. I said partnership."

"So, what, you'll offer me a small percentage of the profits?"

"Damn it, Allie, are you going to keep trying to read my mind—and doing it badly, I might add—or do you want to hear the proposal?"

"Sorry." But she didn't look sorry. "I'm listening."

"We're good together. We each have skills the other lacks."

"You mean, I can navigate, find fish and cook, and you can drink expensive beer and talk about the stock market with the good ol' boys?"

"You're not doing a very good job listening."

She clamped her mouth shut.

He started again. "What I propose is a full, fifty-fifty partnership. My cousins and I won't contest Johnny's handwritten will if you'll agree—"

"You want me to just hand over half my business?"

"Look at the big picture, Allie. With my input, and that of Reece and Max, Remington Charters will earn twice as much as it did before."

"You don't know that."

"I've worked in business for a lot of years, Allie. Reece and Max and I—we know what we're doing. We've turned several businesses around. Of course we don't have guarantees, but we can make an educated guess.

"But there's another reason a partnership makes a lot of sense."

"What's that?"

"It's this thing between us. We're good together in more than a business sense, and you know it. I want to see where it goes."

"Oh my God." She stared at him with a dawning look of horror on her face.

"What?"

"So that's what all this is about. I should have known."

"All what?"

"This!" She stood and made a sweeping gesture with her hand, encompassing their breakfast and the entire suite. "You planned it from the beginning—the fancy clothes, the fancy hotel suite. You set out to make me feel like Cinderella at the ball. Then, when you got me all softened up, you spring this partnership thing on me."

Her attack was so blatantly unfair, Cooper was for once in his life utterly speechless. He was known for his ability to cleverly negotiate no matter what kind of nasty surprises the opposition lobbed at him, but this one feisty redhead had rendered him mute.

"With you lawyer types, it's all about the bottom line. Win at any cost. You know you're going to lose your bid to crack Johnny's handwritten will, so it's on to Plan B. Fifty percent is better than nothing, plus you get a built-in galley slave and free sex. And when you get tired of me? You'll find some legal maneuver to get rid of me."

She walked right up to him and poked his chest with her finger. "I have been down this route before. I fell for it once when I was a teenager, but I won't be a sucker again. So you can just keep your *generous* offer. I will take my chances with the courts."

By the time Cooper came up with a defense, she'd already flounced out of the room and into her own bedroom. He stood in front of the door she'd slammed in his face, devastated.

"It *was* a generous offer!" he yelled. "Because I'm going to win. I was trying to save you some heartache, but it appears you don't *have* a heart!" He paused and listened, but all was quiet on the other side of the door. "Allie?"

He heard the shower go on.

With a sigh he returned to their half-eaten breakfast, but he certainly had no appetite for it now.

After what they'd shared, how could she believe the whole thing was a calculated scheme? He would have to be the coldest, most soulless bastard in the world to cook up a plan like that.

In his experience, innocent people assumed others were as honest as they were. It was only the crooks and cheats who believed everyone was out to get them.

What did that say about Allie?

ALLIE SOMEHOW GOT THROUGH the rest of the day. She did all her crying during a very long shower, so that when she emerged from her bedroom an hour later she was dry eyed, showing as little emotion as possible.

Cooper was obviously angry, too. His every movement was filled with tension, his mouth nothing but a thin, tight line and his eyes sparkling dangerously if she so much as looked at him.

At the trade show they spoke to each other only when absolutely necessary, each of them alternating between the booth and the floor so they didn't have to be together.

It was the longest day of Allie's life.

Unfortunately, they didn't repeat their success from the previous day. Maybe it was the fact that outside the gorgeous spring weather called, or maybe it was the tension in the air, but they signed up fewer than half the number of people they'd attracted on Saturday.

Max showed up to help them pack up at the end of the day. "So, how'd it go?" he asked.

"Fine," Allie and Cooper said in unison, each of them sounding as if they'd just been through a root canal.

"Gee, sorry I asked."

Allie was immediately contrite. She didn't know if Max was in on the plan, but she shouldn't automatically assume he was. "Sorry, Max. It's been a long day. We did well yesterday but today was slow and I'm afraid Cooper and I got on each other's nerves."

"Hey, it happens."

Allie busied herself taking down the fish cutouts. From the corner of her eye she saw Cooper and Max conferring about something, and she guessed it was her because Max glanced her way every now and then. She wondered what sort of spin Cooper was putting on the weekend's events.

It was dark as they climbed into Cooper's car for the drive home. "Do you want to stop somewhere for dinner?" Cooper asked, his tone grim, telling her exactly what he thought about sharing a meal with her.

She was hungry, but she wouldn't be able to eat a bite sitting across the table from him. "No, thanks." She put on her seat belt, reclined the cushy leather seat, and closed her eyes. If she was lucky, she would fall asleep and the drive would be over in no time.

But Cooper had other ideas. "How are we going to run the cruises if we aren't speaking to each other?"

"I can do it alone," she grumbled.

"That's not what we agreed to do."

"Cooper, surely by now you know I'm not going to make off with the boat."

"I don't think I know you at all. And you clearly don't know me if you think I would seduce you just to get my hands on your boat. If I wanted a boat that bad, I could buy one."

"Then why don't you? Why does it have to be this boat?"

"It's a matter of principle."

Allie hooted at that one. "Principle? You're a lawyer. You don't actually expect me to believe that, do you?"

"No, I don't. Because you're determined to believe the

worst of me no matter what the evidence says. Some people think I'm jaded and overly suspicious of everyone, but lady, you take the cake."

"I have every right to be suspicious. My uncle stole my birthright from me. He took my father's boat, left to me in his will, and he sold it without my knowledge or consent. I won't let that happen again."

"You're not the only person in the world to be taken advantage of," he said, his words soft, no longer angry.

She wondered what had made him say that, but she wasn't sure she wanted to know. However, she found she no longer had the energy to argue.

"I will do my best not to rile you up when we have to work together," she said. "Maybe Max or Reece could stand in for you."

He surprised her by laughing. "I'd pay money to see that."

They rode in silence for a while, but then Cooper's phone rang. He didn't answer.

She opened her eyes. "Shouldn't you get that? What if it's a potential customer?" Allie's phone had rung a couple of times today with people wanting more information about Remington Charters.

"It isn't."

A few minutes later it rang again, and again he didn't answer. She wondered what *that* was about.

SOMEONE TAPPED SOFTLY ON Allie's bedroom door at the B and B. She'd been about to climb into bed, but she froze and her heart raced wildly as her traitorous imagination wondered if her visitor was Cooper.

"Allie, it's me, Sara," came a hoarse whisper.

Well, that answered that question. Allie felt like an idiot

as she walked to the door and opened it, summoning a smile for her friend.

"Where've you been?" Allie asked. She'd been surprised that Sara wasn't home when she and Cooper had arrived back at the B and B about an hour ago.

"Date, perfectly awful, not worth discussing." Sara let herself in and promptly plopped on Allie's bed. "So spill it. How did your big weekend with Cooper go?" Sara's eyes sparkled with mischief, making Allie wonder if her friend was psychic. How else would she have known that it was anything but a business trip to work a trade show?

Allie had already decided she wouldn't rehash her stupidity with Sara. Some things were best forgotten as quickly as possible, though how Allie would ever forget the feel of Cooper's touch, she didn't know.

"It went fine. We gave away a lot of brochures and signed up people for a drawing. The booth looked great."

"And…?"

"And nothing." But Allie couldn't meet her friend's inquisitive gaze.

"You mean to tell me you went away for the weekend with that gorgeous hunk of man who practically salivates every time he looks at you, and nothing happened? Do you not have hormones or what?"

Oh, she had hormones, all right.

"Allie? You better tell me what happened."

Allie sighed and flopped onto the bed on her stomach, grabbing one of the pillows and scrunching it under her head. "It was the best and worst weekend of my life."

Sara clapped her hands as she hopped onto the bed. "I knew it!" But then she sobered. "Sorry. All that was for the 'best weekend' part. Was it dreamy?"

"Mm-hmm."

"That's all I get? C'mon, Allie, I haven't had dreamy sex in so long I've forgotten what it's like."

Allie raised her head. "You?"

"Well, you don't have to act like I'm a major slut. Yes, I was a bit wild in my youth, but I've calmed down considerably in my old age. No more cozying up to guys I couldn't possibly have any future with."

"But that's the thing, don't you see?" Allie said. "Cooper and I couldn't possibly be together in the future. When someone's beaten you in court and deprived you of something you believe is yours, how can you even exist in the same room with them?"

"Do you think he's going to win?" Sara whispered.

"No! I think *I'm* going to win. If the judge were to rule fair and square in Cooper's favor, I might get over it enough not to hate him. But I'm afraid the reverse isn't true. Cooper is the kind of man who expects to win. He'll hate me when all this is over."

"You don't know that for sure. Maybe you guys could work it out somehow. Share ownership or something."

Allie raised her head and peered suspiciously at Sara. "Have you been talking to Cooper?"

"What? No. I came straight in here as soon as I got home. Why?"

"It's just that he proposed the exact same thing. He bought me those beautiful clothes, he put me up in a luxury suite at the Hotel Alexander—"

"You stayed there? I'd give up all my Guns n' Roses CDs to stay there!"

"Sara, focus. He wined me and dined me, he…took

care of me when I got a little freaked out about a small fire at the hotel—"

"The Alexander burned?"

"Just a couple of rooms." Truthfully, she'd forgotten about how understanding he was during that incident. That couldn't have been part of his evil plan. Even Cooper couldn't risk burning down his family's hotel just to put her in a vulnerable situation so he could look like a hero. And he'd been so sweet when she'd injured her finger, going out and getting her bandages.

She refused to dwell on that. "Then he cinched the deal by…by seducing me—"

"Oh, Allie, don't be so Victorian. You can't tell me you weren't a willing participant."

Allie bit her lip, trying not to remember how utterly wanton she'd been. "Okay, yes, I did my part. But you're missing the point. By this morning I was nothing but a glob of quivering goo, and then he springs it on me—as if it had just occurred to him. He proposed a fifty-fifty partnership."

Sara stared at her blankly. "And…?"

"Don't you get it? He buttered me up, then tried to catch me in a weak moment. He planned it from the start."

Sara scratched her head, her brow wrinkled in thought. "Let me get this straight. The man dumps a bunch of money into your business with no guarantee of any return."

"Because he expects to win," Allie insisted.

"Fair enough. He's so sure he's going to win that he invests thousands of dollars into your business. He whisks you off to Houston, puts you up in the acknowledged best honeymoon hotel in town, wines you and dines you—did you wear the dress, by the way?"

"As a matter of fact, I did. I assume you had something

to do with that, and I'm not sure whether to thank you or curse you, but it did come in handy."

"Okay. So he wines you and dines you and you have great sex with him—I'm assuming it was great sex, right?"

Allie nodded miserably. She couldn't lie about that. Not that she was any expert when it came to bedroom Olympics, but there was no mistaking good sex when she had it.

"And after all this, he offers you fifty percent of a business he's positive he's going to own, anyway. Do I have it right?"

"He was hedging his bets. He's trying to get half my business because he…thinks…" Oh, hell. There seemed to be a large error in her thinking.

Sara smiled triumphantly. "Exactly. All of his actions have indicated that he thinks he's going to win the *Dragonfly*. So why would he offer you fifty percent?"

"I…I just don't know. But he must have an angle."

Sara picked up a pillow and whomped Allie on the head with it. "You dolt! What were you thinking?"

Allie sat up. "I don't know! He got me all confused."

"No, it's that rat fink uncle of yours who messed you up. He's the one who was out to grab everything he could from you, legally or not. But that doesn't mean every man is out to do the same. I'll admit, it's suspicious how the Remingtons haven't shown their faces in Port Clara until there was money and property involved. But something tells me this situation is not all black and white."

## Chapter Thirteen

Allie had hoped that by showing up at the breakfast table as early as possible, she would miss Cooper and his cousins. But no such luck. The man hadn't slept five hours over the weekend, yet he looked as polished and alert as always, decked out in his yuppie casual.

His cousins were with him, and their heads were bent together in whispered discussion that halted the moment she entered the dining room.

Max was the first to offer her a smile. "Morning, Allie."

"Good morning, Allie," Reece chimed in. "Cooper says the trade show went very well."

Allie selected a chair as far as possible from the Remingtons. "I think so. I've never done a trade show before, so I have nothing to compare it to. But people seemed interested, thanks to Max's video and brochures."

"It was pretty basic stuff," Max said. "I could have done better if I'd had more time. But I'm glad they went over well."

Allie returned her attention to Reece. "So, how's the audit going?"

"Almost done," he said with an uneasy smile, eyes

flicking to the kitchen door. "You keep very good records. Do you have any accounting experience?"

Allie laughed. "No, I never went to college or anything. I just keep the books the way my dad taught me. Johnny's wife—your aunt Pat—had a pretty good system set up. Johnny had made a mess of it after she died, but I got it straightened out."

Cooper looked up at her then. He'd been studiously ignoring her, but now there was no doubt where his attention lay. Nor was there any doubt as to his feelings toward her this morning. Animosity shot out of his eyes like fireworks on the Fourth of July.

"I'll bet you did."

So, they were back to being suspicious that Allie was some kind of gold-digger con artist. She ignored his baiting comment as Sara entered the dining room with a tray laden with all kinds of tasty goodies. She set plates down in front of each of the Remington cousins in turn.

"Denver omelet for Max, fresh fruit and oatmeal for Cooper, and a Belgian waffle for—" Somehow, the plate with the waffle managed to slip out of her hand and fall straight into Reece's lap. "Oh my God, I'm so sorry!" She squealed as Reece bolted out of his chair. She grabbed a napkin and tried to wipe the syrup off him but he quickly took the napkin away from her.

"It's okay, Sara, accidents happen."

"I'll make you another one. I'm so sorry. I'm not usually so clumsy."

No, she wasn't. Sara had served a lot of drinks and meals over the years with her frequent waitress gigs. She was one of the most graceful and self-possessed people Allie knew. So why had she just become a blithering idiot?

"Maybe you should just get me oatmeal and fruit," Reece said as he bent to collect the waffle from the floor. Sara bent down at the exact same time and they clunked heads.

"Oh my God!" Sara bleated. "I'm not usually such a klutz!"

"It's okay, really. Don't worry about it. I'll just go change clothes." Reece made a hasty exit from the dining room, and Sara, looking utterly horrified, quickly collected the dish and the spoiled waffle and hurried back into the kitchen.

Max burst out laughing. "What was that?"

Cooper just shook his head, seeming faintly amused.

Was it possible Sara had a crush on Reece? She'd said something about him being cute and that she wanted to muss his hair, but Allie hadn't taken much notice. Sara thought a lot of men were "cute." Reece didn't seem her type at all. She was much more likely to fall for some itinerant coffeehouse guitarist or a professional surfer than a CPA. In fact, out of the three cousins Allie would have picked Max as a more likely match for Sara.

Sara returned a couple of minutes later looking sheepish. "Allie, I forgot all about you. What would you like for breakfast?"

Allie gave Sara a knowing smirk. "Toast and coffee is all I need, thanks. I overindulged while I was out of town. On food." Clearly Cooper interpreted a broader meaning. Now he was the one offering up a knowing look.

She hastily averted her gaze. Damn the man. He was six feet away, and she could still feel the effects of his eyes on her.

Allie bolted her food as quickly as she could, then wiped her mouth and prepared to make her escape.

"Just a moment, Allie." It was Cooper.

Oh, God, what did he want now?

"Yes?"

"I have some tasks for you today," he said. "I'll expect you to report to work by eight-thirty."

The nerve! She wasn't some serf he could order around. He was angry and he was getting his revenge by acting like…like Captain Bligh. She started to tell him where he could get off—but stopped her runaway mouth just in time.

She kind of deserved his shabby treatment. She was still uncertain what had motivated him to suggest a partnership, and she wasn't a hundred percent sure he wasn't trying to manipulate her somehow. But she strongly suspected he hadn't deserved the tongue-lashing she'd given him the day before.

She should probably be relieved he still wanted anything to do with her. She turned and gave him a smart salute. "Yes, sir. I'll be right back. I just want to freshen up. Are my clothes appropriate, or do you want me to change into something else?"

"Uh, no, you look fine."

As she left the room, she took some small satisfaction in the utter bafflement in his eyes.

"COOPER."

What was Allie up to? Cooper wondered. Yesterday she'd been ready to tear his throat out. Today she was Little Miss Submissive.

"Cooper!"

"What, Reece? You don't have to yell."

"If you can tear your thoughts away from Allie for a

moment, I was about to tell you the results of my audit," Reece said, drawing Cooper back to the present. "I discovered a few interesting things."

"I wasn't thinking about Allie," Cooper blustered, though of course he had been. He couldn't go thirty seconds without thinking about her and wondering what went so terribly wrong. "So what did you find out?"

Reece had stacked Allie's paperwork on an empty chair against the wall, and from it he retrieved a ledger book and opened it.

"First of all, Allie keeps meticulous records. This ledger goes back three years, and she's the one who's made most of the entries. Every once in a while Johnny made a notation, but mostly Allie's the one keeping the books."

"Okay, then." Cooper rubbed his hands together. "She probably took over the bookkeeping the moment she hooked up with Johnny. That would fit with a con artist."

Reece shook his head. "The charter service was providing a good living to both Johnny and Allie until Johnny got sick. Then more and more expenditures went toward doctors and hospitals, and less money was coming in from the charters.

"It appears Allie was socking most of her salary away in her personal account. But the last couple of years, she started to raid her own savings to pay for stuff—boat repairs and maintenance, mostly."

Reece reached for the checkbook and opened it to the relevant entries.

"What? Are you sure?" Cooper peered at Allie's neat, precise handwriting. Reece had flagged checks she'd written related to the business, and there were dozens of them.

"Yes. Not only has she not been embezzling or mismanaging the funds, she's been putting her own money into the business. The financials give *her* ammunition, not us. And if we win, she'll expect these investments to be returned to her somehow."

"How much?"

"Close to fifteen thousand dollars."

Cooper wasn't worried about the amount. It was small, compared to the value of the boat and the business. But he wondered about Allie's motives.

"Looks like she expected all along to inherit the *Dragonfly*," he ventured.

"No, Cooper. What it looks like is a woman who genuinely cared about Johnny and his business and didn't want it to go bankrupt. It looks like she was functioning as a full de facto partner."

"If they didn't have anything on paper—"

"They did. A will. We have to face it—it was Johnny's intention to give this boat to Allie. Now you're the legal hotshot, so we might be able to get it away from her based on legal technicalities, but if we do, that makes us thieves, no better than Heather. I, for one, recommend we drop all legal proceedings."

Cooper shook his head. After all he'd put into this venture? The thought, the money, the legal stuff? He'd quit his job, burned his bridges and alienated his entire family for this dream. Not only that, he'd dragged Max and Reece into it with him.

He wasn't going to just walk away.

"Why don't we try again with the cash settlement?" Max suggested. "Knowing what we do about what she's invested in Remington Charters, we could offer more."

"The amount doesn't seem to be in question," Cooper

said. "I didn't get as far as naming a dollar figure. She shot me down within thirty seconds."

"Everybody has their price," Max said, polishing off the last of his hash browns. "We just have to find Allie's."

Cooper already knew. No amount of money was going to move Allie, at least not any amount he and his cousins could come up with, and they could come up with quite a bit.

Maybe the best thing to do was let the courts sort it out. If he and his cousins won, he would voluntarily pay Allie back her financial investment and then some, enough that she could start fresh somewhere else. If she wasn't a con artist, or even an opportunist, he refused to take away everything she cared about and leave her destitute.

If Allie won—and he had to acknowledge the possibility, since none of his strategies for breaking the handwritten will were panning out—he would have to fall back on Plan B.

Of course, he didn't have a Plan B, but maybe it was time to come up with one.

One thing he wouldn't do, under any circumstances, was crawl home and beg for his job back. He would never hear the end of it. His mother still called him almost every day, pleading with him to see sense and come back home.

His older brother, Derek, would lord it over him if he ever returned to Remington Industries. His life would be a living hell.

As if on cue, his cell phone rang. He checked the caller ID, winced, and let it roll over to voice mail.

"Is it your mom?" Max asked.

Cooper nodded. "Are your parents bugging you to come back?"

Max shook his head. "No way. They're giving me the silent treatment." He sighed. "It's heaven."

"Oh, that reminds me," Reece said. "Derek called."

That got Cooper's full attention. "Derek called you? Why?"

"He couldn't get you to answer your phone."

Cooper should have known he couldn't duck his brother forever. "What did he want?"

"Beats me. He just said to tell you to call."

This was bad news. Very bad. He and Derek had always gotten along fine—until they'd started working together. Cooper's last promotion hadn't sat well with Derek. He'd always assumed the vice presidency was locked up once their father retired, but with Cooper on the rise, he'd become extremely defensive and condescending.

Cooper hoped that his departure from Remington Industries would solve the problem, but he wasn't at all sure it would.

"Listen," Cooper said, "Derek can't get wind of our legal snafu or he'll start stomping around in it, trying to *rescue* me." The possibility turned Cooper's stomach. People said Cooper was ruthless, but Derek made his little brother look like a puppy by comparison.

"Then you better keep Allie away from him," Max said. "Something tells me she won't keep secrets on your behalf."

THE JOB COOPER GAVE ALLIE was the most tedious thing she could imagine; she had to call back every single person who had left either of them a message regarding booking a fishing trip and try to schedule them.

She hated the phone, hated selling. She would have preferred being ordered to scrub algae from the *Dragonfly*'s hull. But she knew it had to be done if she wanted maximum benefits from the trade show, so she buckled down and prepared to jump into the task. She found herself a comfortable chair in the parlor, propped up her feet on a cushy footstool, and settled in to listen to the messages on Cooper's phone first.

"What are you going to do while I'm toiling away on the phone?" she asked since he was obviously planning to go out. He had his car keys in his hand and his coffee in a travel mug.

"I thought I would check on the *Dragonfly*'s progress. We really need to get her back in the water."

"Oh, I wouldn't do that," she cautioned him. "Otis does great work, but he's meticulous and a bit slow. If you bug him, he'll slow down even more. He hates to be rushed."

"I won't pressure him. I just want to see—"

"By showing up, you'll pressure him."

But as usual, he ignored her advice and went his own way. He would learn.

Allie made a list of the names and phone numbers of everyone who had called. Sprinkled among all the messages were calls from someone named Derek who insisted that Cooper return his call; the messages became more insistent.

The final message in the queue was from Derek again: "Derek. Listen, Sylvia and I have decided to come down there and see for ourselves what you're up to. Mom's afraid you've driven your car into a ditch, and that's why you're not answering. We'll arrive tomorrow and stay a couple of days—you can take us fishing on that tub you inherited. If it's everything you've made it out to be, I can put Mom's mind at ease."

Hmm. Obviously Cooper had a brother. And it sounded as if his family wasn't gung ho about Cooper's life taking such a radical turn. Which meant Derek was a potential ally for her.

She checked the schedule, then called Derek back. She got his voice mail, of course. He was no doubt some bigwig at Remington Industries, the type who never answered his own phone.

"Derek, this is Allie Bateman with Remington Charters. We'd be delighted to have you and Sylvia as our guests on a half-day fishing charter on Wednesday afternoon, our first available opening."

They had a trip scheduled for that morning, but it was a short one.

"I'll make a reservation for you at the Sunsetter Bed and Breakfast for Tuesday and Wednesday night," she continued, "but you can extend it if you like." She left the Sunsetter's address and phone number and hung up, feeling a little guilty over her deviousness.

Trying to outmaneuver Cooper had become a nasty habit. If she were really a good person, she would apologize for her bad behavior yesterday even if there was no hope of restoring a friendly relationship.

On the other hand, if they were now destined to fight for the *Dragonfly* to the bitter end, she still intended to win. Even if winning meant she would never see Cooper again.

## Chapter Fourteen

Cooper returned to the B and B feeling pretty pleased with himself. Otis Sinclair hadn't seemed at all bothered by Cooper's appearance, and the work on the boat was almost done. Otis had assured Cooper they could pick up the boat tomorrow morning, which would give them a day to prepare for their first charter, scheduled for Wednesday morning.

The other job he'd commissioned—the repainting of the sign that hung over the *Dragonfly*'s slip—was almost done, too.

He felt confident that once Allie was back on her boat, back in her comfort zone, she wouldn't be so prickly. Her accusations against him still stung, and he hadn't entirely forgiven her for them. But the two of them had to put their differences aside. They had customers to please, plans to implement. The new and improved Remington Charters needed to be running smoothly by the time the tourist season got into full swing.

When Cooper returned to the B and B he found Allie exactly where he'd left her, but looking more tense.

"Is there a problem?"

"Not exactly."

"Did someone give you a hard time?"

"No, nothing like that. In fact, I got four more bookings and several people who said they'd call back after they firmed up their vacation plans."

"Then what's the problem?"

"Not a problem," she said, jumping to her feet. "It's just that you never mentioned your brother Derek."

Cooper went very still. "I don't know that I've talked much about my family to you. How do you know about Derek?"

"He left several messages on your phone. He's coming to visit and he wants to go fishing."

"Fishing?" Derek had never fished in his life.

"He said he wants to go fishing," she said again. "I scheduled him and Sylvia—his wife?"

Cooper nodded numbly.

"I scheduled them for Wednesday afternoon and reserved a room for them here. I hope that's okay."

"Derek. Fishing." Why did Cooper find that a bit hard to believe? Cooper's older brother was the least outdoorsy person he'd ever known. Even as a kid, Derek hadn't been interested in any sport but hockey, always at an indoor arena.

And Sylvia. He'd never seen her out of high heels. She couldn't even sit at an outdoor café without complaining about the heat or the glare or the wind. How would she handle several hours on a boat?

He'd like to think his brother was extending the olive branch by coming to visit and supporting Cooper's new venture. But given how he'd sneered at the idea of Cooper running a fishing business, that didn't seem likely.

In fact, he was pretty sure he knew what was behind Derek's sudden desire to vacation in Port Clara. Their mother's fingerprints were all over it. She was sending

Derek to check up on Cooper and find the weaknesses in this situation, so he could exploit them and convince Cooper to return home properly chastised.

If he tried to convince Derek not to come, it would only make him more determined to get on a plane.

"Did I do the wrong thing?" Allie asked. "I thought you would want me to be nice to your family."

Of course Allie wouldn't know of the rivalry between him and his brother because he'd never mentioned it. "I really would have preferred that my brother visit another time," he said carefully as he made his way to a Victorian love seat and sank into it. "My family was against the idea of me moving down here to run Remington Charters. They thought we should sell the *Dragonfly* and be done with it."

Allie sat on the other end of the love seat. "So you didn't leave New York on the best of terms with them?"

"They'd have done just about anything to stop me," he admitted. "My father believes there's strength in numbers. He thinks of the Remington family as some modern-day dynasty, and if I'm not a hundred percent with him, I'm against him."

"Don't tell me—he's a lawyer, too."

Cooper nodded. "So is my brother."

"I could call Derek back and tell him I made a mistake, that I don't have any openings. I could suggest he reschedule for another day—sometime after our court date."

Cooper was frankly surprised Allie would make such a concession. "Who did you say you were when you talked to him?"

"I just said I was with Remington Charters. I didn't say I was your partner or co-owner, if that's what you're worried about."

The tightness in his stomach eased. That was exactly

what he'd worried about. How would he explain a partner to Derek?

"Will the *Dragonfly* be ready by Wednesday?"

"Otis said tomorrow at noon." He cleared his throat. "Listen, Allie, I know you don't owe me, but I need to ask you a favor. When Derek and Sylvia get here, could you…could you maybe not mention Johnny's other will?"

"How will you explain my presence?" She wanted to know. Clearly she wasn't prepared to disappear for two days. Not that he could ask her to do that. He wasn't ready to run the boat by himself yet.

He didn't suppose she would pretend to be his girlfriend. "You could be my navigator."

She laughed at that. "Navigator?"

"Derek knows nothing about fishing. We could tell him you're my official fish-finder, and he probably wouldn't question it."

Cooper held his breath. If Allie was looking for a weakness she could exploit, this was it. One word to his brother about the *Dragonfly*'s disputed ownership, and Derek would probably throw every resource he had toward helping Allie win. Not that the elderly lawyer she'd hired wasn't doing a decent job, but neither he nor Allie had the resources of the Remingtons.

"You're asking me to lie," she said.

He could have tried to sugarcoat it, but with Allie it was no use. "Yes." He resisted adding that he could make it worth her while. His tendency to break everything down to dollars and cents was one reason Allie mistrusted him.

"Tell you what," she said. "I'll decide after I meet him how much he ought to know."

"Fair enough." Cooper felt a sliver of optimism. He

could predict with ninety-nine percent certainty that Allie would dislike and distrust Derek on sight. He was arrogant, controlling, and wore a sense of entitlement like a crown prince wore ermine—all of which were qualities Cooper shared, though Cooper liked to think his were balanced by a sense of humor and a shred of compassion for his fellow human beings.

Seeing that Allie had softened her angry stance toward him—and he'd mellowed a bit, too—he almost tried to talk to her again about their weekend together. If he could convince her he hadn't cooked up some plot to defraud her, would she let him get close again?

Fortunately, the timely arrival of the UPS man prevented him from opening his mouth and doing something stupid.

"Two packages for Cooper Remington," the delivery-man said.

"That's me." Cooper signed for the packages, one small, one very large. As he brought them inside, he saw Allie watching him with undisguised curiosity. "What's that?"

"Find a box cutter, and you can open it yourself," he said with a hint of teasing in his voice. He couldn't wait to see what she thought.

Allie disappeared, but a few moments later she came back with a butcher knife.

Cooper took a step back from the box and held up his hands. "I'll do better, I promise. Just don't hurt me with the knife."

"Ha ha. I couldn't find a box cutter." She sliced into the carton. Piles of packing peanuts overflowed onto the carpet as she pulled back the lid, and she yanked more of the messy stuff out by the handful until she saw the contents. "A telescope?"

"For the Champagne Stargazer cruises."

*"Stargazer?"*

"I got a brainstorm, and Max changed it on the brochure at the last minute."

"Ah. No wonder so many families have been interested. I've never seen a telescope this big before." She struggled to lift it out of the box.

He grabbed on to it and she pulled the box and the rest of the clinging foam peanuts off the gleaming black instrument. It was a thing of beauty.

"Will it work on a boat?" she asked. "I mean, it's not like we can hold the boat still, even in calm water."

"It's equipped with an image stabilizer," Cooper explained. "But I've also ordered some smaller, handheld telescopes—since only one person at a time can look through the big one. And check these out." He used the knife to open the smaller package, extracting the contents and holding them out for Allie's inspection.

"Glow-in-the-dark star charts. Cool. I think I had one of these when I was a kid."

"I've still got mine." The thing was in tatters, he'd used it so much. Not that he could see all that much from the roof of the apartment building where he'd grown up in Manhattan. The stars were a lot more visible here in Port Clara, away from air and light pollution.

"You like stargazing?" she asked cautiously.

"I did when I was younger," he answered just as cautiously. "I majored in astronomy my first semester in college, but my father convinced me it wasn't that practical so I switched to prelaw."

"That's sad."

"It is?"

"If astronomy was your passion, you should have been encouraged to pursue it. Like me and fishing," she added pointedly.

He shrugged. "I had lots of passions—don't most kids? I don't regret going into law. It was a good, solid career and it provided a comfortable income for a lot of years."

"That sounds like your father talking to me."

Cooper hated that she was right.

"Do you know enough about the night sky to be our resident expert?" she asked. "If you've been advertising a stargazer cruise, people are going to want a knowledgeable guide."

"With a little bit of study, sure."

A yelp caused them both to turn toward the doorway, where Sara stood looking horrified. "I just vacuumed that carpet an hour ago, and guests are due to arrive any minute."

"We'll clean it up," Allie said hastily as she dropped to her knees and scooped up the debris, stuffing it into the now-empty box.

Cooper knelt down beside her to help. "Sorry, Sara."

Their hands brushed as they both reached for the same pile of peanuts, and they both pulled back self-consciously.

"Hey, Cooper," Allie said.

"Yes?"

"Can we try the telescope out tonight? Miss Greer's patio has a pretty good view of the sky."

Cooper's chest ached looking at her face, flushed and excited, reminding him of the way she'd looked when they'd made love.

"Sure. We can make a party of it, and I can try out my tour-guide-to-the-galaxy skills." He wasn't sure why Allie was acting more friendly, but he wanted to encourage it.

Not that he dared take it any further than friends; they'd already proved that romance and business formed a volatile mixture. But he didn't want her as an enemy.

His cell phone rang, breaking the spell that had briefly descended over them. He broke eye contact with Allie and went to answer it.

At almost the same moment, Allie's phone, lying next to his, sang out that she had a call. With a mutual shrug, they picked up at the same time.

"Cooper Remington."

"Remington Charters, Allie Bateman."

"This is Agnes Simms," a woman's voice spoke into Cooper's ear, "Clerk of District Court 3. You requested that we schedule your hearing as soon as possible, and we've had an unexpected opening in Judge Isaacs's schedule on Friday at two p.m. Will that work?"

Cooper's heart lurched. In New York it took weeks, sometimes months, to get anything scheduled in court. He'd had no idea matters could move so swiftly. Still, he saw no real reason to delay.

"Yes," he said, his voice only slightly ragged. "That works for me."

As he disconnected, Allie concluded her call and looked up at him. The look in her eyes startled him—part fear, part resignation, and a little bit of sadness.

"You agreed to Friday?" she asked.

He nodded. "But if you need more time—"

"No. It's a simple enough case. Let's just get it over with. The uncertainty is killing me."

AFTER HER DUTIES WERE FINISHED for the day, Allie walked down to the marina for an early dinner of fish and chips.

She sat on a bench on the short boardwalk and stared out at the ocean. Usually the sight of the waves, ceaselessly chasing each other and washing up on the beach with a roar, soothed her and allowed her to gather her thoughts.

But today, nothing was going to soothe her.

Part of Allie wished she'd dragged her legal problem out another couple of weeks, just to see where this thing with Cooper could go. When they'd been unpacking the telescope, she'd almost forgotten the rift between them as she'd envisioned those stargazing cruises.

In her mind's eye the tableau had unfolded: their guests reclining on deck chairs, maybe bundled up in sweaters if it was a cool evening, kids busily studying their star charts and peering into the sky, Cooper showing them how to use the telescope and finding planets and nebulas for them to look at, excited exclamations as they recognized constellations and planets or looked at the moon's craters for the first time.

But with the judge's decision coming on Friday, she and Cooper wouldn't be doing the cruises together. If Cooper lost, he would take his telescopes with him. She could probably get Sara to help her do the evening charter, but it wouldn't be the same.

And if she lost… Oh, God, she didn't want to think about it. She hadn't even let herself consider the possibility of actually losing everything she'd built up over the past ten years.

A battered old seagull landed on a post, eyeing her lunch with interest. Normally she didn't feed the gulls: if you did, they just became worse pests than they already were. But something about this scarred veteran, who'd obviously survived many a storm and maybe a predator or two, tugged at her heart, and she tossed him her last two French fries.

"Maybe that's a farewell gift," she said before he flew away, instinctively knowing she had nothing else to offer.

LATER THAT NIGHT, COOPER set up his new telescope on the patio and everyone wanted to check it out. Even Miss Greer, who'd been spending a lot of time in her private sitting room due to an arthritic hip bothering her, came out to see what all the chatter was about.

Cooper had invited all of the B and B's guests to join in, which included his cousins, Sara, and a fifty-something pharmaceutical saleswoman from San Antonio named Martie. Sara made up a batch of sangria, which transformed their gathering into a true party.

Not that Allie was in much of a partying mood. She sat off to the side, sipping the potent punch and watching as Cooper reacquainted himself with the night sky, consulting some books he'd checked out of the library.

He was a bit subdued as well, she noticed. But she could tell he really did enjoy astronomy and knew more about it than the average joe. In fact, he had a lot of interests she wouldn't expect a lawyer to have. Once when she'd gone for a walk on the beach at dawn, she'd seen him there, too, not running to get his morning exercise but strolling at a leisurely pace, pausing often to look out at the sea, and picking up the occasional seashell or bit of ocean glass.

She had to admit he was really nothing like what her first impressions had led her to believe.

Allie let herself envision, for one brief, dangerous moment, how different things would be if she'd accepted Cooper's partnership offer, if she hadn't been so suspicious and paranoid.

Sara came and sat next to her. "Hey, you okay? You're awfully quiet. Is Cooper giving you trouble?"

Allie shook her head. "Actually, he's been pretty decent given how I acted yesterday. But the hearing's been set. Friday."

"So soon?"

"It's better to get it over with."

"Yeah, but I was hoping if you two spent more time together, you'd realize you were meant for each other."

Allie smiled. "Sara, you are such a dreamer."

"But it's true. Cooper's been making cow eyes at you all night. I think he's fallen in love with you, and who could blame him? Why don't you just tell him you made a mistake?"

She'd considered it. "If I change my position so drastically, he'll assume it's because I'm about to lose my business."

"Only if he's as suspicious as you are."

"He is." It was something else they had in common. Maybe not their nicest shared trait.

"Maybe when it's all said and done, then," Sara said. "You won't have anything to lose by trying."

But Allie was afraid Cooper wouldn't be a good sport about losing. He was clearly used to being on the winning side. Even if he tried not to be a sore loser, how could he avoid resenting her for stealing his inheritance?

Resentment would poison their future dealings so that any relationship, even friendship, would be out of the question.

"Allie, come look at Saturn," Cooper said suddenly, startling her.

"O-okay." She stood, set down her glass, and walked across the patio to the telescope. She bent down to peer through the eyepiece.

"It's beautiful," she barely breathed. The planet's rings were clearly visible. She'd never seen anything like this outside of a book.

"Yeah, it sure is."

She straightened to find Cooper staring at her, not the sky.

## Chapter Fifteen

"I made a reservation to fly home tomorrow," Reece announced casually as he drove Cooper and Allie to Sinclair Marine. Otis had called to let them know that work on the *Dragonfly* was complete.

Cooper was more distressed than he cared to admit that Reece was going home. Then again, his cousin had been acting a bit cool since learning that Cooper intended to go forward with his legal case.

In the back of his mind, Cooper had been convinced that Reece would find it so pleasant to be away from the pressures of his corporate accounting job that he would change his mind and elect to resign and move to Port Clara permanently.

But his cousin had been on the phone almost constantly, putting out fires back home or going over spreadsheets e-mailed to him. Some vacation.

"You're not even staying for the hearing?"

Reece glanced into the backseat at Allie, who was plugged into her iPod, tuning them out. "Only if you want me to testify on Allie's behalf. You have my written statement indicating the results of the audit."

Cooper hadn't realized how strongly Reece felt about

this. He would have to talk to him, make sure his cousin understood he wouldn't leave Allie high and dry. He wanted to do what was fair. Really, he did.

But he would have to save his arguments for when Allie wasn't around.

Reece pulled Cooper's BMW into the Sinclair Marine parking lot, where Cooper and Allie got out. Allie pulled out her earphones and stuffed her iPod into her jeans pocket without a word. She'd been quiet last night, too. He knew the possibility of losing the *Dragonfly* must weigh heavily on her. It did on him, too.

Otis greeted them with a big smile. "Nice to see you folks again. I got her all spiffed up and ready to go. Want to inspect her before we settle the bill?"

Cooper started to say yes, but Allie spoke first. "I'm sure your work is perfect, Otis. Let's get the bad news over with."

They all crowded into Otis's tiny office, where he rummaged around on his messy desk until he found the itemized bill. Cooper got his hands on it first, but Allie was right there peering around his shoulder.

"Oh," she said. "Um, Otis, isn't this a bit more than we agreed on?"

"No, ma'am," he said confidently. "The cost for repairing the hull damage is exactly what I quoted you. The rest is for the painting Mr. Remington here ordered."

"The what?" Allie grabbed the bill from Cooper and inspected it more closely, then she looked up at him with a thunderous expression. "You had painting done on the boat without talking to me first?"

"You'll like it, I promise."

Her expression said she doubted that.

He'd really wanted her to see the results before the bill.

"Don't worry, I'll pay for it." He was already handing Otis his credit card.

"That's not the point," she said, folding her arms. "We're partners, at least until Friday. We're supposed to make decisions together. And how am I going to pay you back for all the money you've invested in Remington Charters? I assume you'll want some return on your investment if the judge's decision doesn't go your way."

"Allie, I told you before that I don't expect you to pay me back anything. Putting money into the business was my decision, my risk. We never put anything on paper, therefore I have no legitimate claim."

"That's how you would see it, I suppose," she said stiffly, though some of the starch had gone out of her. "Others of us do business on the honor system."

"I thought I was making an investment in myself. But maybe it wasn't the smartest risk I ever took." He never thought he'd be admitting that to Allie, but it was the truth.

"You think you're going to lose?" she asked, sounding confused.

"Don't you?" he countered, rather than answering her.

Impatience replaced her confusion. Did she think he was trying to trip her up?

With the repairs paid for—and another hit to his Visa, which could take a lot of abuse but not indefinitely— Cooper and Allie headed out to the dock to have their first look at the revamped *Dragonfly*.

Cooper, however, had his eyes firmly glued to Allie. Her reaction would say a lot about her.

When she gasped, he knew she'd seen it and understood the scope of the work he'd had done.

"Oh my God, Cooper, what did you do?"

"If we're going to bill ourselves as offering luxury cruises, our boat has to look the part. The *Dragonfly* is a great old tub, and she deserves to look her best."

The *Dragonfly* did, in fact, look the best she'd looked since she was new almost thirty years ago. She'd been painted stem to stern. Anything that hadn't been painted had been scrubbed clean as a whistle. The canopies had been replaced with bright-blue striped canvas.

Allie climbed on board and walked around, reverently touching various parts of the boat, her face reflecting nothing short of wonder. "I wouldn't even recognize her if I didn't know... Lord, Cooper, you didn't buy a new boat, did you?"

Cooper joined her on deck, laughing. "No, it's the same old *Dragonfly*."

Allie opened the hatch and went inside, where the changes were less obvious. But Cooper had replaced the carpet and the refrigerator, which had been on its last legs.

"There's something else I want you to see," Cooper said as he opened the hatch that led to the boat's underbelly and gave access to the engines.

Allie stared down into the hole, where her spaghetti bowl of wires was conspicuously absent. "How did you do this?"

"Jim Jameson recommended his mechanic to me. He charges more than Mickey, I imagine, but he overhauled all the wiring—in fact the whole electrical system. We can't have the engines refusing to start at some inconvenient time."

Allie turned to Cooper, her eyes shiny with tears. "Oh, Cooper, thank you, thank you!" She threw her arms around him and hugged him like she never wanted to let him go.

Well, that was an abrupt U-turn.

Cooper's arms slid around her and held her close. God,

she felt so good, so right against him. Her hair smelled like something tropical and exotic, rubbing soft as a dream against his cheek.

He had to make things right between them. Somehow, he had to get her to trust him. Maybe he hadn't yet earned that trust, but he would work to earn it, and he wouldn't give up.

Allie pulled back just enough that she could look at him. "Thank you for doing this," she said again. "Johnny hated to see the *Dragonfly* looking shabby, and he would be so pleased, so proud to see her so beautiful. Even if I have to walk away on Friday, I'll feel better knowing you're taking care of her the way Johnny would have wanted."

"I have a lot to make up for where Johnny's concerned." He could never undo the fact that he hadn't tried harder to mend the rift with his uncle. The only thing he could do now was try to carry on the fishing business in his memory.

"Wherever he is," Allie said, "I bet he's watching. And I know he's forgiven you for anything you feel you might have done wrong."

Cooper understood now that Allie was none of the things he'd suspected of her. She'd loved Johnny, not as a lover and not just as a friend or employee, but as a daughter would.

Cooper was afraid of saying the wrong thing, so he settled for kissing her on the forehead and releasing her. If he could have he would've bundled her into the captain's quarters and showed her just how he felt about her. But Otis had appeared in the hatch, his forehead wrinkled with worry.

"Everything okay in here?"

Allie went to him and hugged him, too, making Cooper feel just a little bit less special. "Oh, Otis, everything is beautiful. I wish Johnny was here to see it."

"Me, too, honey. Port Clara lost a great man when

Johnny Remington passed over. But I know he'd be pleased to see how you're carrying on, so strong."

"If I'm strong, it's because he made me that way."

Damn. Cooper had a lump in his throat, and he was going to start boohooing any minute if they didn't stop talking about Johnny.

"Maybe we better get going," he said, his voice gruff. "We have a lot of work to do before our first charter tomorrow morning."

IT WAS ALL ALLIE COULD DO not to weep with joy as she piloted the *Dragonfly* back to the Port Clara Marina. The engines sounded better than they had in years, and if Allie didn't know better, she would say the boat was riding a bit perkier in the water, almost as if she was proud of her makeover and wanted to show it off to all the other boats.

Cooper hadn't joined her on the bridge, choosing instead to sit at the bow, his legs dangling over the side as he held on to the railing and faced into the wind.

Maybe he was giving her time alone to say goodbye.

She never should have convinced herself she was going to win. She had no legal expertise, after all, and only a small-town lawyer to help her out. Cooper, on the other hand, knew the law, and he'd been confident of his success from the very beginning. She'd been wrong to dismiss that confidence as arrogance or bravado.

Now she had only a couple of days to come to terms with the loss. But knowing how Cooper cared for the boat and for Johnny, maybe the loss would be easier to swallow.

As they eased the boat into her slip, Allie saw Jane was back, puttering around on the deck of her beautiful boat.

This time Kaylee, her three-year-old daughter, had come with her. The darling blond-haired little girl stood at the railing, looking like a beacon in her bright orange life jacket.

She hopped up and down and waved frantically when she caught sight of Allie. "Allie, Allie! Mommy, look, Allie!"

Jane turned and her face registered a smile of recognition, though Allie couldn't help noticing that she appeared strained even from a distance.

"Ahoy, you!" Jane called as she came to the railing and rested her hand on the top of Kaylee's head. "Oh my gosh, the *Dragonfly* looks fantastic!"

Cooper busied himself tying off the lines, so Allie descended the ladder and hopped onto the dock. She joined Jane on the *Princess II.*

"Hi, there, flipper!" she said to Jane's daughter, who was the light of Jane's life. Allie privately thought that Kaylee was the only thing keeping Jane sane, given the oaf she was married to. Allie picked up Kaylee and held her aloft as the child squealed in delight, then gave her a hug and set her down.

"Where did you disappear to?" Allie asked Jane. "I thought you guys were down for the whole weekend, and then suddenly you were gone. I hope nothing's wrong."

"Actually, something's right, or about to be," Jane said with cautious optimism. "I haven't wanted to talk about it, but Scott and I are getting divorced. In fact, it will be final in two weeks."

"Oh, Jane, I'm so sorry." Although really, Allie wasn't sorry at all. Scott Simone was a monumental jerk. But any divorce was difficult. Separating spouses had to admit defeat and failure of their marriage, which probably had started out with great hopes and expectations. "What about

Kaylee?" It would be just like Scott to fight for custody, simply to be hurtful.

"I have full custody, thank God. Scott asked for one weekend a month. Can you imagine?" She lowered her voice and whispered in Allie's ear, so Kaylee wouldn't hear. "That's all he wants to see his daughter. Ten-to-one he won't even want that, and it'll be just as well. Kaylee will be better with no father than one who clearly doesn't put her first."

Allie couldn't agree more.

Jane resumed talking in her normal voice. "We came down here last weekend for one last-ditch effort to work things out, to see if we could remember why we'd gotten married in the first place. But when Scott punched out Max Remington, that was it for me. He was insanely jealous of any male who even talked to me, no matter what the circumstances. It was only a matter of time before he started hitting me instead of the supposedly flirting men."

"So Max wasn't flirting?"

Jane looked embarrassed. "Well, he was flirting a little. I suspect a man like Max Remington simply can't help himself. When he's near anything female, he flirts. It oozes from his pores."

Jane's gaze flickered to behind Allie, where Cooper still puttered around. "I'm dying to know what's going on. Can you stay for lunch? The *Princess II* is all mine now, to do with as I please. It's the sum total of my settlement."

Allie was appalled. Scott Simone had been worth millions.

Jane laid a hand on Allie's arm. "No, it's what I wanted. Full custody of Kaylee is the only thing that mattered to me. I don't want Scott's money."

"But how will you live?" Allie asked. "You aren't going to sell the boat, are you?"

"I'll keep it if I can. At least it's a roof over our heads, and I have a little cash to tide me over until I can find a job. I'm fine, really."

"All right," Allie said. "But if you need anything, I'm right next door." At least for three more days.

Allie returned to the *Dragonfly,* where Cooper had found himself a deck chair and was looking pretty satisfied with himself.

"I thought you said we have a lot of work to do." She nudged his Top-Sider with her foot. "We at least need to lay in some provisions for tomorrow. I assume you want something a little fancier than cold cuts for your brother."

"Can we do fancy?" he asked. "I've made a lot of bold promises, but quite honestly I've been planning to hire someone to do the food and drink."

"I got it covered," she said with a grin. "If Miss Greer can spare Sara, I'll ask her to help. We'll knock your brother's socks off."

Cooper returned her smile, but suddenly his face froze as something caught his eye behind her.

"What?" Allie asked, whirling around, and that was when she saw him. The very brother in question, as if she'd conjured him up by mentioning him.

Allie could have picked him out of a lineup—even a lineup of corporate lawyers—because he looked just like Cooper. A bit taller and rangier, perhaps, but he had the same blue eyes, the same prominent nose, same yuppie weekend-casual wardrobe.

As he strode purposefully toward the *Dragonfly,* his eyes took in every detail as his brain processed them— evaluating, assessing. His mouth firmed, as if he didn't like what he saw.

"Cooper." He gave a stiff wave.

"Oh, God," Cooper said under his breath. "Here we go." He looked briefly at Allie, silently begging her not to spill the beans.

She'd already made the decision that she wouldn't tell Derek the real story of how she and Cooper had come to be working together on the boat. In fact, she would let him be captain-for-a-day. She would handle food-and-beverage duty, and let his brother see for himself that Cooper had made a wise decision, that he was living the good life.

Cooper met his brother on the dock while Allie hung back, doing her own assessment. "Derek." The two men shook hands. Not very warm and cuddly. But then, not all families were raised to be huggers. She cautioned herself not to make any snap decisions about Derek Remington, as she'd done with Cooper.

"Where's Sylvia?" Cooper asked his brother.

"Unpacking at the B and B. She'll join us later." Derek's gaze roved over the *Dragonfly*. "So, *this* is what dragged you away from your home, your family and a six-figure income. The way you described it, I thought it would be bigger." He glanced up and down the dock, taking in the other boats, probably comparing the *Dragonfly* to her neighbors. His gaze settled briefly on the *Princess II*. Probably the pleasure craft was more to his taste.

Allie silently vowed that by the time Derek returned to New York, he would be ready to turn in his resignation at Remington Industries and sign on as a deckhand working for Cooper.

"This is the *Dragonfly*," Cooper said proudly. "Isn't she the most gorgeous thing you've ever seen?"

Obviously not, as he made no reply.

"Come on board," Cooper said with a tad less enthusiasm. "I'll show you around."

As Derek stepped aboard, his critical gaze fell on Allie, who waited politely to be introduced. He eyed her with interest, probably trying to guess who the hell she was.

"Derek, this is Allie Bateman, my…" He stopped, clearly not wanting to lie outright.

Allie decided to do it for him. "I work for Cooper."

"In what capacity?" Derek asked, shaking her hand, his smile distant.

"I'm his fish-finder," she said, and Cooper slapped his hand over his mouth to stifle what she hoped was laughter. "Best in the business. I'm also a gourmet chef, and I prepare all the meals for our passengers."

"Ah. You can get me a cold beer, then."

"Yes, sir. Right away." Gawd, he did everything but snap his fingers at her and say, "Chop chop." And she'd thought Cooper was arrogant.

Fortunately, Otis had moved what little food and drink had been in the old fridge to the new one, so she was able to lay her hands on a cold beer.

"So, who is she really?" Derek asked, his body language reeking with disapproval.

Allie stopped when she realized they were discussing her. She stood there, frozen, not sure whether she should retreat, interrupt them, or eavesdrop.

She decided to eavesdrop.

"She is, in fact, the best fish-finder on the Texas coast," Cooper said. "And she works miracles in the galley."

"So she's not your little playmate?" Derek asked. "Mom wondered if there wasn't a woman involved, given your history of turning stupid around a pretty girl. Heather wasn't the first woman to take advantage of you."

Oh? This was interesting. What awful thing had Heather done? Was that what made Cooper so suspicious?

"No, we're not involved," Cooper said.

*Not anymore,* Allie added silently.

"But I'll agree she's pretty."

"If you like that earthy, tomboy look. You didn't, last time I checked."

Allie gasped. How rude. Then she remembered she wasn't supposed to be listening. She stepped through the hatch and rejoined the men, handing Derek his beer.

"There you go, sir."

"Thank you," he said without looking at her.

"Captain Remington," she said to Cooper, "I was just on my way to buy provisions for tomorrow's outings, so I'll leave you and your brother to visit."

Cooper bit his lip. "See you later, then."

As she disembarked, he mouthed a silent *thank you.*

COOPER HAD BEEN HOPING FOR more time to prepare for his brother's visit, but at least Allie was playing along. He wasn't sure why it even mattered. So what if Derek thought he was insane for wanting to fish for a living? But all his life he'd been competing with his brother—partly thanks to the fact their father always pitted them against each other—and he couldn't bear the thought of Derek returning to Manhattan with tales of how deluded Cooper was and what a mess he was making of his life.

"So this is for real?" Derek asked. "I figured you'd play around on the boat for a week, then put it up for sale and come home."

"That's not going to happen," Cooper assured him. As he did, something tight uncoiled inside him. He didn't have to worry anymore whether Derek approved. Derek had no power over him—none. The resentment he'd felt for his brother vanished like the morning mist and with it had gone any need for subterfuge.

Cooper took a deep breath. "Allie isn't really my fish-finder, although she's damn good at finding fish. She's my partner." Man, it felt good to say that. "Johnny wrote a new will, awarding her the *Dragonfly*. She has a legitimate claim, and she's sunk her life savings into this tub. It's all being sorted out in court Friday, but until then we're working together to keep the charter business going."

Derek looked at him as if he'd just announced he ate small children for breakfast. "I *knew* you'd come down here and gotten yourself into trouble. What time is the hearing? I'll have to rearrange my schedule—"

"No, Derek. I don't want you there."

"Do you want to keep the boat or not?" Derek asked, utterly baffled.

"I do. But I want to keep the girl, too."

ALLIE WAS QUITE PLEASED with their morning charter the following day. She'd spent the previous evening preparing ingredients for a slightly more upscale breakfast for the two men and one fourteen-year-old boy who were their passengers. Everyone, including Cooper, devoured the sausage-and-egg wraps, which bore no resemblance to the fast-food version of the same dish. Allie's exploded with the taste of fresh herbs and real aged cheddar cheese.

They were fishing for barracuda, and the fish were being elusive, but the men didn't seem to care. And when the boy caught the one and only fish of the day, he came unglued he was so excited, and the two men coached him on how to bring in the big fish. So all in all it was a good trip.

As soon as the passengers were gone, she and Cooper got to work cleaning and straightening and preparing for Derek and Sylvia's visit. But Cooper seemed relaxed about the whole thing.

"Oh, by the way," he said, "I told Derek everything. He knows about the two wills, and the fact we're partners."

"Really. What was his reaction?"

"He thinks I've gone 'round the bend. Which maybe I have. Allie, tell me honestly. When I first got here, was I like him?"

"I'm afraid so." When she saw the disappointment on his face, she gave him a break. "Okay, you were only somewhat like him."

"By moving down here, I might have saved myself just in time."

After all the build-up, the cruise with Derek and Sylvia was anticlimactic. Sylvia was about what you'd expect a corporate lawyer's wife to be—beautiful and polished and well-spoken, polite to the extreme but reserved.

The couple wasn't terribly interested in fish, but Cooper baited their hooks and put their lines in the water, anyway. And when Sylvia's line went taught, the haughty look disappeared from her face and she squealed with excitement.

Allie watched from the bridge as Cooper coached her on how to bring it in. She fought it for nearly two hours, and by the time she brought it in—a good-sized sailfish, of all unexpected things—she was sweaty and sore and sunburned, and she declared it was the most fun she'd ever had in her life.

As Cooper piloted the boat toward home, Derek and Sylvia ate the chicken tarragon salad on croissants and steamed asparagus Allie and Sara served, raving about it the whole time.

The two of them left Port Clara totally sold on fishing and promised they would return in the fall for a longer visit.

Allie wondered which one of them, her or Cooper, they would find running Remington Charters.

## Chapter Sixteen

Friday came way too soon.

Allie and Cooper had a morning charter, and ironically it was probably their smoothest and best ever. The three male passengers spent most of their time upping each other, seeing who could bring in the most snapper. Their wives, however, were far more interested in Allie's cooking, going so far as to invade the galley to find out how she was making those delicious wraps.

As she worked, Allie was keenly aware of the fact this was her and Cooper's final cruise together—and possibly her last outing on the *Dragonfly*.

She took the bridge on the way home and left their passengers to Cooper's capable care. "Well, Johnny, I gave it my best shot," she said, knowing the drone of the engines and the wind would drown out her voice. "The truth is, I'm not sure I could've made it on my own. If Cooper wins, he'll do you proud."

As the boat neared port, Allie mentally recorded every detail of the experience—how the wind felt against her skin, the smell of the salt air, the way the sun sparkled on the water.

It all felt different since Cooper had come into her life. She would find a way back on the water, that she knew. But it would never be the same.

After they'd seen their passengers off, Allie barely had time to return to the bed-and-breakfast—she hadn't yet moved back onto the boat, since she might have to move right back off—and grab a shower. She dressed in the white outfit for court, since it was the only thing she owned remotely appropriate, but she wore a high-necked black shirt underneath so as not to flash her cleavage.

She met Arlen Caldwell in front of the courthouse. He'd caught a cold, and he sneezed into a giant handkerchief every couple of minutes.

"So what do you think?" Allie asked the elderly attorney. "Are we going to win?"

"As I've said from the beginning, the law's on your side," he answered. "It all depends on what kind of tricks that shyster from New York tries to pull. But Judge Isaacs is no dummy. He won't be taken in by smoke and mirrors."

Allie smiled at Arlen's description of Cooper as a shyster. She'd have said the same thing a few weeks ago.

Cooper's BMW pulled into the parking lot, and that was her cue to hustle Arlen inside. She hadn't seen him since they'd parted ways after the morning charter; they'd managed to avoid each other at the Sunsetter. If she saw him now she might lose it.

Once they were in the courtroom, she planned to simply not look his way.

The courtroom wasn't like she pictured it. For one thing, it was tiny. The judge sat behind a normal-looking desk, not one of those giant, imposing things she'd seen on TV. A small table was set up for each party in the dispute. A half-dozen folding chairs accommodated anyone else interested in the proceedings.

Allie and Arlen took their places behind their table; Cooper, Reece and Max filed in right behind them and sat at theirs. They all wore sober suits, even Max, though unlike his cousins he appeared ill at ease in his, tugging often at the collar. Apparently Reece had postponed his trip back to New York.

Sara showed up, too, looking like a colorful butterfly in her paisley-print skirt. She gave Allie a little finger wave and found a chair.

Cooper looked Allie's way, and she quickly averted her gaze. Darn it, she said she wasn't going to look at him. Her throat was already tight, and if she was required to testify she feared her voice would come out sounding like Minnie Mouse.

"Are both parties ready to start?" Judge Isaacs asked.

"Yes, Your Honor," Cooper said. Lord, even speaking those three simple words, his voice rang with sincerity.

"We're ready, Your Honor," Arlen said. His voice was scratchy, and he sneezed again into his handkerchief.

"I've read both wills cover to cover," the judge said, "and I've read the depositions provided by both parties. Mr. Remington—Mr. Cooper Remington, that is—you're representing yourself and your cousins, is that correct?"

"Yes, Your Honor."

"Did you have anything to add at this time?"

"No, Your Honor. I believe the documents speak for themselves."

Allie nearly fainted. A lawyer who didn't want to stand up and pontificate when he had the chance?

"Mr. Arlen Caldwell, have you anything to add?"

Arlen stood. He opened his mouth, seemed to think better of it, and closed it again. "No, Your Honor, I concur with Mr. Remington. The documentation speaks for itself."

"Then I'm prepared to render my decision."

Now Allie really did feel lightheaded. So soon? She'd expected some kind of recess, during which the judge would ponder the facts before announcing the verdict. But since neither party added new information today, he must have already known how he was going to rule.

That didn't mean she was ready for it.

Arlen, sensing her distress, patted her hand reassuringly.

"The handwritten will," the judge began, "appears to be legal in every respect. Since the date on this will supersedes that of the other will, it takes priority. Therefore, I am awarding full ownership of the boat known as the *Dragonfly,* and everything on it, to Ms. Allison Bateman."

Allie closed her eyes. Just like that, it was over, and she'd won. She'd expected to feel triumphant at this moment, but she felt a curious emptiness inside.

"However," the judge said, and Allie's eyes flew open, "the handwritten will makes no mention of the business known as Remington Charters, Incorporated. The earlier will, however, specifically spells out Johnny Remington's wishes in regard to that business, which is a separate legal entity from the boat."

What? Allie glanced over at Arlen. He looked suddenly worried.

"Therefore," the judge continued, "I hereby award ownership of the corporation known as Remington Charters to Cooper Remington, Reece Remington and Maxwell Remington, to be shared equally among them. Allie Bateman, you will cease and desist using the Remington Charters name or logo, and you will turn over ownership of any corporate bank accounts and all records pertaining to the business, and the fruits of any contracts you entered into under the Remington Charters name, to Mr. Cooper Remington, representative for all three Remington parties."

The judge droned on and on about how if she didn't follow his orders in a timely fashion, a representative of the court would step in then. But her ears were buzzing so loudly she couldn't hear.

Her first thought was to suspect Cooper of somehow engineering this disaster. But when she glanced over at him, she could see he was just as stunned as she was. The Remington cousins were all staring at each other, slack-jawed.

The judge ended the hearing, but Allie just sat there, because she didn't think her rubbery legs would hold her up.

"I guess I should have seen this coming," Arlen said in a low voice. "But I'd always thought of the boat and the fishing business as one and the same."

"You aren't the only one. Even Cooper didn't anticipate this decision."

"We can appeal," Arlen suggested.

But Allie couldn't stand the thought of dragging this out any further.

She couldn't start a fishing charter business from scratch, not without a huge influx of capital. On the other hand, Cooper would have a hard time running a fishing business with no boat. He would have to buy a new one.

She knew what she had to do. But she wasn't ready to do it.

"Send me a bill for the remainder of what I owe you," she said to Arlen. "It may take me a little while to pull my finances together, but you'll get paid."

"Now, now, I told you not to worry about that. But I do have one more matter to take care of." He reached into his jacket and extracted a sealed envelope with her name on it. "Cooper came to my office yesterday. He asked that I give you this once the hearing was over, no matter which way it went."

She was almost afraid to touch the envelope. "What is it?"

He shrugged. "I have no idea. But I'm curious as hell," he said with a twinkle in his eye. "The boy seemed agitated when he gave it to me."

She glanced over at the opposing counsel's table, but Cooper and his cousins were already gone.

Allie slipped away from the courthouse through a back door, fearing she would run into Cooper otherwise. She only went to her car when she was sure the Remingtons were gone.

But she didn't return to the B and B. She drove to the beach. She wanted to read the letter somewhere where no one could see her, because she suspected it was going to make her cry.

Anyway, she did her best thinking near the ocean, where the sound of the waves crashing on shore soothed her and the smell of salt air cleansed her mind.

Port Clara's public beach was small. Soon the tourists would cover the sand with their towels and umbrellas, but today it was cloudy, windy and deserted. Not the best sunbathing weather, but it suited her mood.

Allie took off her shoes and walked barefoot in the warm sand, then sat at the base of a sand dune, letting the natural surroundings calm the roiling inside of her.

She pulled her knees into her chest and propped the letter across them, staring at her name. She was terrified to open it.

She'd have to sell the *Dragonfly* to Cooper. Or maybe, if he didn't have the capital to buy it outright, she would lease it to him. The one thing she wouldn't do was hold on to it out of spite. If she did, she might kill off Johnny's legacy for good.

She wasn't sure how long she'd been sitting there, minutes or hours, when a shadow moved over her.

"Do you know how long I've been looking for you? I was afraid you'd gone and drowned yourself."

Cooper.

"I appreciate your concern," she said, meaning it, because he really did sound distressed. "Is that the effect you thought your letter would have?"

"I hope not," he said with some alarm. "Have you even read it?"

"I haven't. But I really need to do that alone."

"Yeah, well, it's a public beach and I have every right to sit and watch the ocean." He sat down beside her, and she was surprised to see he was wearing a disreputable pair of cutoff jeans and an Old Salt's Bar & Grill T-shirt. He looked a lot more beach bum than corporate lawyer.

"I suppose you want me to pay you back for all the money you put into the *Dragonfly*."

He sighed. "No, Allie, for the third and final time—I hope—you don't owe me anything. If you would just read the damn letter, you would know what I'm thinking."

"The decision surprised you?" she asked, stalling.

"Yeah. I feel like an idiot for not anticipating it. I'm supposed to be the hotshot lawyer around here."

"Are your cousins upset?"

"Truthfully? They both think the judge should have given it all to you. Johnny's intentions were clear, even if there was a slight oversight in his will."

"And what do you think?"

"I think the boat's no good to you without the business."

"And the business is no good to you without the boat," she countered. "Which is why I'm offering to sell you the *Dragonfly*. It's the only solution that makes sense."

He appeared truly surprised. "You'd do that?"

She nodded, resigned but sincere. "Johnny wouldn't want it all broken up."

Cooper frowned. "I hate to burst your bubble, but I don't have the money to buy a boat. I've put almost all my liquid assets into Remington Charters already."

Now she was the one who was surprised. She'd been thinking of Cooper as having an endless supply of cash. "I could lease it to you until you're ready to buy."

"Actually, I have another idea. But I don't want to get my head bitten off again."

She put her face in her hands, deeply regretting the drama-queen hissy-fit she'd thrown in Houston. "I'm really sorry about that," she mumbled between her fingers. Then she looked up at him. "I understand now you weren't trying to cheat me or manipulate me. You really were trying to find a solution that would benefit everyone."

He shrugged. "I'm not *that* honorable. The truth is, when I proposed the partnership, I was looking for some way we could be together. I didn't want to lose you. But I ended up saying the one thing that would alienate you for good."

Allie was touched at the vulnerability in his voice. How could she have gotten it so wrong? "I wasn't alienated for good," she assured him. "Sara made me come to my senses. But I figured by then I'd burned my bridges." She paused, hoping he would deny she'd done any such thing.

But he didn't.

"Cooper, who's Heather?"

He looked surprised at the mention of the name. "How did you hear about her?"

"I overheard Derek say something about her when I went in to get him a beer. I wasn't listening on purpose, but I couldn't help hearing."

Cooper took a deep breath. "I was once engaged to Heather. She ripped me off for close to a quarter million dollars before disappearing into the night."

Allie gasped. "That's horrid! Did you put her in jail?"

"No. She got away clean. I imagine she's happily fleecing some other sucker by now."

Allie knew how it felt to be fleeced and betrayed by someone who was supposed to love you. But Cooper was the last person she would call a sucker.

"Would you read the letter?" he said impatiently.

"You were going to tell me your idea for solving all our problems."

"It's in the letter. But it's so obvious, I don't know why you haven't thought of it."

"You…you still want to set up a partnership?" she asked, afraid to hope. She'd figured that possibility was off the table.

"A very special kind of partnership." He took her hand and placed something in her palm, wrapping her fingers around it. It was cold and hard, and it had sharp edges. "Since you won't read the letter, I'll tell you what's in it. It says, Allie Bateman, I love you with all my heart. I think I fell in love with you that first day I saw you, when you threatened to get your gun and shoot me. Would you do me the honor of becoming my wife?"

Allie couldn't breathe. Honestly, she thought she was

going to pass out. Her ears were buzzing and her head felt like it was about to float away from her body.

But then she remembered to inhale, and her vision cleared. She opened her hand and looked at the object Cooper had given her. It was a diamond ring. An enormous square diamond ring.

"I'll give you Remington Charters as a wedding present," he added. "Reece and Max agree."

"Oh, Cooper."

"Is that 'Oh, Cooper, yes'? Or 'Oh, Cooper, get lost'?"

"Oh, Cooper." She couldn't seem to say anything else. She'd never seen this coming. "I mean, yes. I love you, too. Yes." She threw her arms around him with so much enthusiasm it knocked him over into the sand. He laughed, and then he was kissing her and she felt like her entire world had just flip-flopped and she'd landed in the place where all her dreams were coming true—even the ones she'd never admitted she had.


"DAD, I SEE THE BIG DIPPER!" a seven-year-old boy shouted. He stood near the railing with his glow-in-the-dark star chart, trying to identify constellations while Cooper helped his older sister to view the planet Mars.

With all the celebrating, Cooper and Allie had nearly forgotten they had their first stargazer cruise scheduled for that night. But they'd scrambled to get the new telescope mounted and prepare cookies and brownies—and the promised champagne.

Their first stargazer passengers were a family of four from Houston. Allie remembered talking to them at the trade show. They'd been looking for a new and different getaway weekend.

The kids were clearly enchanted with the night sky. The weather had cooperated, providing them with a crystal-clear, cloudless sky. The parents lounged on side-by-side deck chairs, holding hands and sipping their bubbly from plastic flutes.

Navigating the calm waters at night was no problem, and unlike with the fishing cruises, Allie could find a nice spot and throw out the anchor, allowing her to join in the fun.

"Cooper, is that Cassiopeia's chair?" she asked, pointing to five bright stars that formed an M-shape on the southern horizon. She knew it was, but since he was their resident expert, she let him play the part.

"Yeah, it sure is," he answered.

"Where? I want to see!" The boy rushed to Allie's side and peered up where she pointed.

"Me, too," said the girl. Brother and sister got into a good-natured argument about whether it actually looked like a chair or not, and who was Cassiopeia, anyway?

Cooper and Allie drew back into the shadows, and he kissed her softly. The ring winked at her, even in the dim light. She knew it wasn't that smart to wear it while she was working, but she couldn't bear to take it off, not today.

Reece and Max had seemed genuinely pleased when they heard news of the engagement, both swearing they'd seen it coming. Allie insisted they retain a percentage of ownership in the fishing business, but they'd seemed un-concerned about that.

Sara had been over the moon, and she and Miss Greer had fixed a special dinner that night.

"Where should we get married?" Allie asked Cooper, leaning against him in the moonlight.

"Hmm. You're the captain of a boat. Maybe you could marry us right here."

She laughed. "I don't think I could officiate at my own wedding. Besides, I'm not the captain. We're co-captains. The sign says so."

She'd been surprised and thrilled when she'd arrived at dock a few hours ago to see that Cooper had hired someone to repaint the sign over the *Dragonfly*'s slip. The sign had listed both "Captain Allie Bateman" and "Captain Cooper Remington," side by side, with both of their phone numbers.

"You were pretty sure this was going to work out," she commented.

He shrugged. "Not really. But I was hopeful."

"In that case, I pronounce us husband and wife," she said.

"Does that mean tonight's our wedding night?"

"As far as I'm concerned, every night's our wedding night. For the rest of our lives."

\* \* \* \* \*

*Be sure to look for Reece Remington's story,*
*the next book in the SECOND SONS trilogy*
*available in December 2008*
*from Harlequin American Romance!*

*Love Inspired*
**HISTORICAL**

*Powerful, engaging stories of romance, adventure and
faith set in the past—when life was simpler and faith
played a major role in everyday lives.*

*See below for a sneak preview of*
*HIGH COUNTRY BRIDE*
*by Jillian Hart*

*Love Inspired Historical—love and faith
throughout the ages*

Silence remained between them, and she felt the rake of his gaze, taking her in from the top of her wind-blown hair where escaped tendrils snapped in the wind to the toe of her scuffed, patched shoes. She watched him fist up his big, work-roughened hands and expected the worst.

"You never told me, Miz Nelson. Where are you going to go?" His tone was flat, his jaw tensed as if he were still fighting his temper. His blue gaze shot past her to watch the children going about their picking up.

"I don't know." Her throat went dry. Her tongue felt thick as she answered. "When I find employment, I could wire a payment to you. Rent. Y-you aren't think-ing of bringing the sher-riff in?"

"You think I want *payment?*" He boomed like winter thunder. *"You think I want rent money?"*

"Frankly, I don't know what you want."

"I'll tell you what I don't want. I don't want—" His words cannoned in the silence as he paused, and a passing pair of geese overhead honked in flat-noted tones. He grimaced, and it was impossible to know what he would say or do.

She trembled, not from fear of him, she truly didn't believe he would strike her, but from the unknown. Of being forced to take the frightening step off the only safe spot she'd known since she'd lost Pa's house.

When you were homeless, everything seemed so fragile, so easily off balance, for it was a big, unkind world for a woman alone with her children. She had no one to protect her. No one to care. The truth was, she'd never had those things in her husband. How could she expect them from any stranger? Especially this man she hardly knew, who was harsh and cold and hardhearted.

And, worse, what if he brought in the law?

"You can't keep living out of a wagon," he said, still angry, the cords still straining in his neck. "Animals have enough sense to keep their young cared for and safe."

Yes, it was as she'd thought. He intended to be as cruel about this as he could be. She spun on her heel, pulling up all her defenses, and was determined to let his upcoming hurtful words roll off her like rainwater on an oiled tarp. She grabbed the towel the children had neatly folded and tossed it into the laundry box in the back of the wagon.

"Miz Nelson. I'm talking to you."

"Yes, I know. If you expect me to stand there while you tongue lash me, you're mistaken. I have packing to get to." Her fingers were clumsy as she hefted the bucket of water she'd brought for washing—she wouldn't need that now—and heaved.

His hand clasped on the handle beside hers, and she could feel the life and power of him vibrate along the thin metal. "Give it to me."

Her fingers let go. She felt stunned as he walked away,

easily carrying the bucket that had been so heavy to her, and quietly, methodically, put out the small cooking fire. He did not seem as ominous or as intimidating—somehow—as he stood in the shadows, bent to his task, although she couldn't say why that was. Perhaps it was because he wasn't acting the way she was used to men acting. She was quite used to doing all the work.

Jamie scurried over, juggling his wooden horses, to watch. Daisy hung back, eyes wide and still, taking in the mysterious goings-on.

He is different when he's near to them, she realized. He didn't seem harsh, and there was no hint of anger—or, come to think of it, any other emotion—as he shook out the empty bucket, nodded once to the children and then retraced his path to her.

"Let me guess." He dropped the bucket onto the tailgate, and his anger appeared to be back. Cords strained in his neck and jaw as he growled at her. "If you leave here, you don't know where you're going and you have no money to get there with?"

She nodded. "Yes, sir."

"Then get you and your kids into the wagon. I'll hitch up your horses for you." His eyes were cold and yet they were not unfeeling as he fastened his gaze on hers. "I have an empty shanty out back of my house that no one's living in. You can stay there for the night."

*"What?"* She stumbled back, and the solid wood of the tailgate bit into the small of her back. "But—"

"There will be no argument," he bit out, interrupting her. "None at all. I buried a wife and son years ago, what was most precious to me, and to see you and them neglected like this—with no one to care—" His jaw ground again and his eyes were no longer cold.

Joanna didn't think she'd ever seen anything sadder than Aiden McKaslin as the sun went down on him.

\* \* \* \* \*

*Don't miss this deeply moving story,*
*HIGH COUNTRY BRIDE,*
*available July 2008*
*from the new Love Inspired Historical line.*

*Also look for SEASIDE CINDERELLA*
*by Anna Schmidt,*
*where a poor servant girl and a wealthy*
*merchant prince might somehow make a life together.*

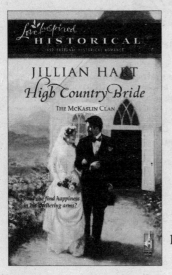

# REQUEST YOUR FREE BOOKS!
## 2 FREE NOVELS PLUS 2
# FREE GIFTS!

*American ★ Romance*®

## Heart, Home & Happiness!

*Silhouette*

# SPECIAL EDITION™

### NEW YORK TIMES BESTSELLING AUTHOR

# DIANA PALMER

A brand-new Long, Tall Texans novel

# HEART OF STONE

Feeling unwanted and unloved, Keely returns to Jacobsville and to Boone Sinclair, a rancher troubled by his own past. Boone has always seemed reserved, but now Keely discovers a sensuality with him that quickly turns to love. Can they each see past their own scars to let love in?

*Available September 2008
wherever you buy books.*

**Visit Silhouette Books at www.eHarlequin.com**   SSE24921

**Harlequin American Romance is celebrating its 25th anniversary just in time to make your Fourth of July celebrations sensational with Kraft!**

# WAVE YOUR FLAG CAKE

| Prep time: | Total hours: | Makes: |
|---|---|---|
| 20 minutes | 4 hours 25 minutes (incl. refrigerating) | 18 servings, one piece each |

*4 cups fresh strawberries, divided*
*1-1/2 cups boiling water*
*1 pkg (8-serving size) or 2 pkg (4-serving size each) JELL-O Brand Gelatin, any red flavor*
*Ice cubes*
*1 cup cold water*
*1 pkg (12 oz) pound cake, cut into 10 slices*
*1-1/3 cups blueberries, divided*
*1 tub (8 oz) COOL WHIP Whipped Topping, thawed*

SLICE 1 cup of the strawberries; cut remaining strawberries in half. Set aside.

STIR boiling water into dry gelatin mix in large bowl 2 minutes until completely dissolved. Add enough ice to cold water to measure 2 cups. Add to gelatin; stir until ice is melted. Refrigerate 5 minutes or until slightly thickened (consistency of unbeaten egg whites). Meanwhile, line bottom of 13x9-inch dish with cake slices. Add sliced strawberries and 1 cup of the blueberries to thickened gelatin; stir gently. Spoon over cake slices.

*(Continued on next page)*

# WAVE YOUR FLAG CAKE *(continued)*

REFRIGERATE 4 hours or until firm. Spread whipped topping over gelatin. Arrange strawberry halves on whipped topping for stripes of flag. Arrange remaining 1/3 cup blueberries on whipped topping for stars. Store in refrigerator.

## Kraft Kitchens' Tips

**Substitute:**
Prepare as directed, using JELL-O Brand Berry Blue Flavor Gelatin.

**Variation: Wave Your Flag Cheesecake**
Prepare cake and gelatin layers as directed. Refrigerate 4 hours or until firm. Beat 2 pkg (8 oz each) softened PHILADELPHIA Cream Cheese and 1/4 cup sugar with wire whisk or electric mixer until well blended; gently stir in whipped topping. Spread over gelatin layer. Continue as directed.

Each Harlequin American Romance book in June contains a different recipe from the world's favorite food brand, Kraft. Collect all four to have a complete Fourth of July meal right at your fingertips!

For more great meal ideas please visit
## www.kraftfoods.com.

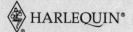

# COMING NEXT MONTH

**#1217 SMOKY MOUNTAIN REUNION by Lynnette Kent**
*The State of Parenthood*
The last time Nola Shannon saw Mason Reed was at her high school graduation. Twelve years later she still carries a torch for the handsome teacher—now a widowed father. And Mason's certainly never forgotten *her*. He and his young son need someone special in their lives. Could the lovely, caring Nola be that someone?

**#1218 HANNAH'S BABY by Cathy Gillen Thacker**
*Made in Texas*
It's the happiest day of her life when Hannah brings her adopted baby home to Texas. But what would make the new mother *really* happy is a daddy to complete their instant family. And Hannah's friend Joe Daugherty would make a perfect father. He just doesn't know it yet!

**#1219 THE FAKE FIANCÉE by Megan Kelly**
What's a man to do when his mother wants him to have a family so badly she ambushes him with blind dates? Hire the caterer to be his fiancée, that's what. His mom is thrilled, but will Joe Riley and Lisa Meyer's pretend engagement become the real thing?

**#1220 TRUST A COWBOY by Judy Christenberry**
*The Lazy L Ranch*
When Pete Ledbetter's granddad decides to find Pete a wife, the bachelor cowboy has no choice but to get his own decoy bride-to-be. He looks no further than his family's Colorado dude ranch. After a summer romance, he knew he was compatible with chef Mary Jo Michaels. But after their summer breakup, he knew winning back her trust would be nearly impossible....

www.eHarlequin.com